NIGHT COURT

NIGHT COURT
by
ASHLEY FONTAINNE
Published by:

RMSW PRESS

Malvern, Arkansas

Copyright © 2015 by Ashley Fontainne

Publisher: RMSW Press, LLC
ISBN-13: 978-0692559819
ISBN-10: 0692559817

Cover and interior design: One of a Kind Covers
Photo credits: Nicolas Raymond www.freestock.ca and Pixaby.com

DEDICATION

For all those who've lost a loved one to addiction

CONTENTS

OTHER BOOKS BY AUTHOR

Novels by Ashley Fontainne
Whispered Pain
Growl
Empty Shell
The Lie – soon to be the feature film FORESEEN
www.foreseenmovie.com
Number Seventy-Five – soon to be a feature film
www.number75themovie.com
Eviscerating the Snake Trilogy:
Accountable to None
Zero Balance
Adjusting Journal Entries
Poetry and Short Story Collection
Ramblings of a Mad Southern Woman
The Magnolia Series:
co-authored with Lillian Hansen
Blood Ties – The Bonds Are Permanent
Coming soon:
Blood Loss
Blood Stain

1

Merry watched, her presence cloaked by the shroud of night.

She'd been outside long enough for her vision to acclimate to the darkness. She missed nothing from her perch against the old brick wall. Her shoulders, back, and legs ached, angry for being stuck in the same position for so long.

They screamed for freedom from bondage.

She ignored them.

Tuned the pleas out—it was as simple as switching off a light switch. Physical pain was a breeze to override. Years of fighting off the aging process by taking up yoga, cross-training, and running, had programmed her muscles and brain to block out body aches and pains. Gave her the internal fortitude to push on, not give up, resist the temptation to cave in and surrender to the burn.

When she took up those activities, she had no idea they would serve a much darker, sinister purpose in her life.

Mental anguish was quite another story. Merry fought

1

hard, refusing to listen to her mind and soul, which in the beginning, begged her to forget the disturbing, insane plans ruminating inside her mind. The urging to not embark upon the journey that took months of sleepless nights to craft.

She taught herself how to push aside the faint voice deep inside, the one pleading for mercy.

To return to sanity.

The last hurdle: a faint whisper to not take the life of another.

Cleared!

That was all in the past now, just like her former life. She'd mastered the art of turning her mushy heart and soul to stone. It was the main piece of the puzzle needed to transform herself into a killer. The thought made her almost giggle out loud at the absurdity of the phrase. On instinct, her gloved hand flew up and clamped over her mouth, just in case a sound escaped her dry throat.

Ha! Murder by Numbers nailed it. I'm living proof of what one must do to become a killer.

Nothing moved except her eyes, which were focused on the night's target. He would be her first execution.

No remorse, no regret.

No second guessing her decision to end the life of a monster who more than deserved the punishment she was about to dole out.

Her actions would smother her old life of suburban housewife and mother, replacing it with—what? Crazed serial killer? The hand of justice?

In the end, did it really matter what others thought or called her?

Not one damned bit.

Muscles tensed and at the ready, her doubts and misgivings had vanished, pushed away by the adrenaline racing through her. The Lycra top wasn't heavy, just hot. It trapped the humid night air against her chest like a vise. A thin bead of sweat trickled down her forehead and perched on the tip of her nose.

She ignored it.

The sounds of the city weren't as loud at three a.m. Traffic from I-30 hummed in the distance. An occasional car horn beeped. Muted voices of the drunks leaving nearby bars and restaurants buzzed around her. Dogs barked, along with the shrill cry of a baby.

Suddenly a siren trilled, making her heart pound, and breathing come faster. Concentrating, she honed in on the sound. No, it wasn't close, and it was fading fast, which meant the cop was heading in the opposite direction. Probably a unit responding to an accident on the highway or pulling over a drunk.

She inhaled deeply, forcing her breath to return to an even, steady rhythm. Merry focused her attention back to the noises around her position. The squeaks of a few rats to her left barely registered. Squeaks which only a few months ago would have sent her running and screaming in the other direction.

Merry ignored it all.

Nothing mattered except completing the mission.

The rational voice whispering in her mind to turn and go home, silenced, banished forever the minute she dressed her five-ten frame in all black—red hair hidden under a skullcap—and left her house earlier. Strength and power flowed through her still torso, fueled by bloodlust. The sensations were much more enjoyable than the gut-wrenching pain of the broken-hearted forty-plus-year old woman she had been.

Merry had waited in the alleyway for almost three hours, camouflaged in black, crammed up against a filthy dumpster. No one except dealers and users ventured into this part of downtown the minute the sun disappeared. The office workers had scattered, unwilling to be caught on the streets after darkness fell. During the past two months of careful plotting, she had learned the habits of the lowlife drug dealer she had marked as her target.

Merry discovered this particular alley was worked only by him.

All her planning, down to every possible scenario, was only seconds away from fruition.

The peddler of death was about to be Little Rock's latest crime statistic.

And he would be Merry Marie Hall's first example of the swift judgment enforced by her own internal court.

Her eyes narrowed into small slits as she watched him saunter into her trap.

Court is now in session. The Honorable Merry Hall, presiding. The defendant, Carlos "Peppy" Ramirez, is found guilty. The punishment for his multitude of crimes is death. Execution shall now be carried out by the Court. The Defendant's appeal is denied. Sentencing to commence. Right now.

Merry bit her lip to keep the snide grin at the corners of her mouth at bay. She watched Peppy's lanky body move with catlike grace through the alley toward her. He was so close she could smell him—a disgusting mix of body odor, chemicals and cheap cologne. He reeked, and the stench assaulted her nose. Less than twenty feet away, he stopped and glanced around.

Merry held her breath.

From her research, she knew Carlos Ramirez had been a street thug for years. Before his twentieth birthday, he'd been arrested over ten times for peddling narcotics. Each arrest and conviction ended the same way: a large fine, no prison time, and a slap on the wrist. A few times, forced attendance at classes that were supposed to teach him how to live life drug-free. He'd be right back on the streets within hours after an arrest and only went to meetings for the free food—and potential of scoring new clients.

How did his public defender sleep at night, knowing his legal finagling allowed a dangerous criminal back on the streets? How did the prosecutors feel each time they came face-to-face with the same exact person for the same exact crimes? Did they feel like they were just spinning their wheels in the mud? What about the judges? Did it ever get under their skin, knowing their courtroom was more like a circus, and they were just shepherding the cattle and sheep in a perpetual circle? Not to mention the heroic cops, who risked their lives every single time they hit the streets. How much time and manpower was spent arresting the wastes of society, only to have to sit back and watch the bastards waltz out of jail?

In.

Out.

In.

Out.

Guilty.

Time served.

Pay a hefty fine.

Keep the county coffers full.

People—no, animals—like Peppy were a threat to society. Leeches that sucked out the life of addicts with each snort, shot, swallow, and injection they sold. Anything could be used as tender: cash, other drugs, sex, or a combination of all three. Peppy, and others like him, didn't care about the age of their clientele or how the poison they offered would condemn the user to a life of sorrow, pain, and grief. They never concerned themselves with what the addiction would do to not only the addict but to those who loved them.

Merry had.

She had relived the nightmare over and over, until it finally drove her to madness. She had been the kind of woman who had a loving husband, adorable son, great job and was living the American dream.

Not anymore.

The idyllic world of Merry Marie Hall, loving wife of Harold and proud mother of her only son, Joshua, was long gone. The disappearing act began the minute Peppy Ramirez sold a little white pill to Joshua nearly five years ago. Watching her child become a raging addict, battling with the court system, (in-out, pay a hefty fine), and depleting their retirement for expensive trips to rehab (which never worked) took their toll on her mental and physical state. The countless arguments late at night with Harold about the situation and the cringing when the phone rang at two or three o'clock in the morning—the signal yet another arrest happened—had aged them both.

Fast.

Almost destroyed their marriage.

Her former life had been finally been snuffed out in less than one week. The flame dimmed six months ago when she heard the news—the night her brother knocked on the front door at three a.m. The minute Merry woke up from the sound of the pounding, she went numb. In the deepest recesses of her heart, she knew Joshua was gone. Felt the hole, the giant black void, gut her chest. She knew before the stoic Detective Derek Isaac Clarke, her tough-as-nails brother, had a chance to say a word. While she sat on the couch, erect and frozen in one spot, hands clasped with Harold's, the hole spread. Engulfed her heart and then overtook to her mind. When Derek told them Joshua was the victim of an overdose of heroin, the blackness began to choke her.

What little light left in her world extinguished when Harold suffered a massive coronary that ended his life at Joshua's funeral.

Not the time to think about things you can't change. Concentrate on your purpose.

She blinked twice and refocused. The time for mourning was over. Carpooler, soccer-mom, devoted wife—she was one with a quick smile and jovial demeanor. Now, all that was gone—buried right next to the corpses of husband and son. What resided inside her now was Maniacal Merry—a woman bent on revenge after her old life ended.

The new one was on the cusp of beginning—one started by the actions of Carlos Fucking Peppy Ramirez.

Merry waited and watched with patience. Not only was Carlos a dealer of just about every conceivable drug, but he was also a heroin user. The combination made him beyond careful. The times she'd followed him in the past, she had to maintain a safe distance. Peppy was on constant edge and wary of his surroundings. The little waste of flesh was intent on guarding his stash and cash from would-be thieves or rival dealers.

Merry could see his shoulders sag a bit, indicating he was satisfied he was safe. Sure enough, Peppy reached into his pocket and pulled out a smoke, lit it, and then leaned back against the dirty brick wall. He was less than ten feet away. The lone streetlight cast eerie shadows across his withered face. The plumes of white smoke looked like horror movie vapors. He wasn't looking in her direction. Peppy's attention was focused on a barking dog at the end of the alleyway. Merry stood and pulled out the syringe from her pocket. Her gaze never left his torso, searching for any movement or signs he'd heard her move.

He hadn't.

Peppy's cell phone rang, startling them all, including the dog. The mutt bounded away into the night, leaving the alleyway quiet again. With a flick of his wrist, Peppy put to the phone to his ear. His raspy voice bounced off the walls straight into Merry's ears.

"Yo, what ails ya? Uh-huh. Yeah, I gotcha back. Always do, right? Stuff is straight, and I mean straight. No cuttin' at all. Yeah, same place. Hurry up. You know I don't hang in one spot too long. Aight? Oh, I hear ya. Ain't we all? If it's a problem, we'll work it out. I know those lips of yours are worth their weight, ya dirty ho. Later."

In disgust, Merry cringed while Peppy rubbed his crotch. The warped smile on his face made her want to vomit.

"Mmm, mmm! Gonna fill her up right! She's worth a few hits for free."

Sliding the cap off the tip of the syringe with her gloved hand, Merry made sure to keep her movements slow and quiet. Peppy finished his smoke and knelt down on the wet cement. Removing his jacket, he fumbled around in the pockets while muttering about his upcoming deal and payment arrangements. His back was to Merry. Her steps were quick and sure. In three strides from her long legs, footfalls silent, the thick rubber on her shoes covered by duct tape, she was behind him.

She wouldn't give Carlos "Peppy" Ramirez a chance to realize what was happening until it was too late for him to do a damned thing about it.

Raising her right leg, visions of her husband and son in their respective caskets, Merry brought it down with all her might. The flat of her boot-clad foot connected with the base of his neck. Peppy made a strange grunting sound as his body jerked forward. His cell phone flew from his hand, clanking on the pavement as it bounced away.

His face slammed into the damp concrete. Red droplets

sprayed into the air as his nose and lips met the ground. He groaned again and tried to roll away.

Merry was faster.

Dropping down, she buried her knees in his back, her full weight centered right below where his rib cage ended. Peppy squirmed underneath her like a worm on hot blacktop in the middle of summer.

Grabbing a handful of Peppy's thin, black hair, Merry yanked his head up, and then slammed it into the ground. His yelp of pain was muffled by the blood in his mouth and throat, and the sound of his teeth shattering. She repeated the movement until his arms quit flailing and no more grunts erupted.

He was out cold.

And his bare arm was exposed.

Can't ask for it to get any better than this.

In one swift motion, she hopped off his back and crouched next to his arm. Finding his vein was simple, even in the dim alleyway. It stood, swollen and ugly from God-only-knows how many years of abuse. Merry held her breath as she buried the needle into it. She pushed the plunger all the way down, releasing the heroin she found in Joshua's apartment months ago into Peppy's body. The empty needle barely made a sound when she let it go and it fell onto the pavement.

Out of breath, Merry scrambled to her feet. She took several steps away from the dealer of death's limp body and picked up his cell phone from its resting place. In seconds, the movements memorized from hours of practice, she opened the back and yanked out the SIM card and shoved it into her pocket.

In three steps, she reached his jacket. She emptied the pockets, taking all the drugs she found. After stuffing them in her waist pack, she tossed the paraphernalia around like confetti.

Peppy let out a slight moan while trying to turn his head. Dropping his jacket, she turned to look at him. His face was covered in dripping, thick red blood, dirt, and pebbles. She couldn't decide what was worse, the gore all over him that she created or the fact it didn't seem to faze her in the least.

Merry moved closer, mindful of the pools of blood surrounding the head of her prey. Flicking open his cell phone, she set it down inches from his bloodied hand. She punched in 9-1-1 but didn't hit send.

"Hey, Peppy. Is this what you want? A chance to call for help before you overdose, or bleed to death from the ass-kicking I just gave you? Hmm? Well, here you go."

She pointed to the phone, though she really didn't know why. It was doubtful he was aware enough to comprehend her words, much less see. "I've even dialed for you. All you have to do is hit the send button. It's right here by your hand. Come on, just reach out and grab it. Help is only a few inches away. Isn't that what you want? What you crave? Help? Someone to rescue you from certain death?"

A slight groan was Peppy's only response.

Every disturbing memory of the last six months flooded her mind.

Standing on the other side of the glass while the coroner pulled back the sheet, exposing Joshua's pale body.

Derek holding her while she crumpled into a blubbering mess on the cold, concrete floor of the M.E.'s office.

Joshua's body lying in the casket.

Her own anguished screams when Harold clutched his chest in agony and fell to the floor, dead before he collapsed next to their son's coffin.

Picking out caskets for the two most important men in her life over the course of five days.

The memories infused Merry with righteous anger. She growled, "Guess what? That's what every single junkie wants, and you don't give it to them. You hand them death instead. Push their salvation away inch by inch with each hit you sell them." The toe of her boot pushed the cell phone out of Peppy's reach. "Just like I'm going to do to you."

With a sick, twisted fascination, Merry watched while the dying Peppy tried to form words. His pathetic attempts to blink and wash away the blood clouding his vision weren't working. His fingers wiggled as they fumbled around for the phone. As the drugs careened through his body, he looked like he'd become one with the blacktop. Blood oozed from his mouth. A bubble of air as he tried to speak popped.

The sounds of heels clacking on the ground caught Merry's attention. The bastard's last deal was close. Instead of finding herself a fix, the woman would turn the corner and discover bloody carnage.

Maybe the sight will help get her clean.

Merry leaned closer, her lips inches away from the monster's blood-soaked ear. "That was for losing my husband. This is for killing my son."

In a flash, she was on her feet. One final stomp to the back of his neck ended the life of Carlos "Peppy" Ramirez with a sickening crunch.

The sound of footsteps drew closer, so Merry quickened her pace. She bent down, grabbed the still-warm index finger which was coated in fresh blood, and scrawled a rival gang's symbol on the pavement to his right.

With that, Merry turned and fled into the night.

One down. Many, many more to go.

2

7 A.M. FRIDAY MORNING

The first hour after arriving home was spent pacing back and forth while waiting for the sound of a knock, signaling her actions earlier had been discovered. When that didn't happen, she showered three times. Finally, Merry sat down at the kitchen table and zoned out, staring out the window into the empty backyard.

She was helpless to stop the ever-shifting scenes that played in the theatre of her mind.

They started with Joshua's birth, watching her beloved Harold while he held their wiggly bundle for the first time. She pictured Harold mumbling through his tears of joy about how much he loved their child, marveling at Joshua's head full of wild, dark brown hair, just like his own. It had been the first time—though certainly not the last—Merry witnessed her spouse cry.

The images shifted to Joshua's first day of kindergarten. How it had taken all her strength to smile and wave goodbye as

Joshua plopped down behind the tiny desk in a tiny chair, his own lopsided grin a mile wide. Once inside the car, Merry cried so hard she had to sit in the parking lot for fifteen minutes.

Zooming forward, she relived the night things changed for the Hall family, though they didn't know it at the time. She saw Harold by her side, each of them sporting black and orange jerseys with *Hall* and the number *27* proudly emblazoned on the back. They sat in the bleachers of the football stadium, alongside Savannah, Joshua's girlfriend of two years, cheering like fools. Harold and Merry watched their seventeen-year-old son, all six-foot-four of him, as he made acrobatic catch after acrobatic catch.

Then, time slowed as the final catch of Joshua Robert Hall, star wide receiver for the Hilldale Charging Wildcats, ended his football career while only a junior in high school. The injury dashed any hope of a college scholarship in mere seconds. The hit was vicious, and in eerie unison, the crowd gave a collective gasp as Joshua's leg buckled under him at an odd, unnatural angle.

She flashed back to the ride in the back of the ambulance with Joshua to the hospital, neither of them remotely considering the accident was the beginning of the end. He'd been as close to a perfect child as one could get—never got into any trouble, made decent grades, and had a heart of a lion. A lump formed in her throat as she relived the vision of the fear and pain behind Joshua's blue eyes. She tried to keep him calm, telling him things would be fine, trying to keep her own fear out of her voice.

Unfortunately, none of those things mattered after Joshua got his first taste of pain killers. With the ability to play sports over, and the future he'd envisioned ever since he'd donned his first helmet in fourth grade, Joshua sunk into a deep depression. Her mind echoed with the memories of how each visit with his doctor while his leg healed, and the assurances made that Joshua's emotional state was normal, and would pass once he's fully recovered.

Stop this. Think. Plan ahead. Acknowledge your first kill. Let it control your thoughts, not the past.

The annoying alarm blared from the cell phone on the kitchen table. Merry stared at it and contemplated throwing it against the wall. In the end, she just reached over and turned it to silent.

She didn't need the electronic reminder to wake up. Sleep had evaded her for two full days. Her nerves still thrummed with the electrical pulse of excitement from killing, the nagging fear of being caught, and the precious memories of an existence no longer alive.

Downing the last sip of coffee, she stood and headed to the bathroom. Her muscles throbbed with each step, as well as the ever-present pressure in her head. Hot water cascading over her body would help alleviate the soreness before she dressed for work.

Uh-huh. Another shower is just going to dry my skin out even more. I don't have but a handful of lotion left to coat my body. No amount of hot water, scented soap, or a rough go-around with a loofah mitt will remove the stain I burned into my soul.

Ignoring her tired, stressed out thoughts, Merry stepped into the shower. Once finished, she used what lotion she had left, dressed, grabbed the plastic bag on the bathroom floor containing her black ensemble, and exited the bathroom. Out of habit rather than interest or curiosity, she flicked on the TV. She needed background noise while she attempted to conceal the dark circles under her eyes.

Got to keep up appearances—look normal. Everything is fine in the world of Merry Hall.

Yeah, right.

Grimacing at the annoying internal dialogue with herself, she concentrated on keeping her fingers from shaking while applying makeup. Just as she finished the last swoop of mascara, she heard it. Though she knew she shouldn't be surprised, the news report still made her heart pound. Despite the sickening feeling in her gut, she watched and listened. The somber face of some new blonde reporter she didn't recognize, one wearing too many layers of fake eyelashes, announced the discovery of an as yet unidentified body. The tip-line telephone number of Little Rock Police Department flashed across the bottom of the screen.

Her tight muscles relaxed a fraction when the reporter mentioned "unidentified sources" indicated the man's death "quite possibly" could be gang related.

Zippity freakin' do-da! That last minute idea was golden!

The news amped Merry up more than two cups of espresso. In a flash, she shut the TV off, grabbed her purse and the bag, and headed off to work with renewed vigor and a big smile.

※ ※ ※

"I've decided I'm tired of watching you turn into a stick figure, so I brought us both a healthy lunch today. You will eat it. I won't take no for an answer. Oh, and no more running out for fast food at lunch. Eat crap, look like crap. That is, if you are actually eating while out."

Merry watched Debbie with wary eyes. Her friend packed the fridge in the office kitchen full of some sort of vibrant green salad, topped off with strips of chicken. The effort made Deb's tight blonde curls bounce in harmony. A few stragglers tumbled around her face and stuck to bright, red lips.

Merry held on to the sigh she wanted to release. Ever since Harold and Joshua died, her weight had steadily declined. The first twenty pounds fell off from not eating due to sorrow and grief. The next ten or so from simply forgetting to feed her growling stomach. She had been too busy researching and planning out her new direction in life. It irked Merry a bit that no one seemed to notice her toned physique. All the rigorous physical training, performed in secret in her garage at night, helped her put on seven pounds of toned muscle.

She notices my weight loss but not my muscle gain?

"How sweet of you, Deb. Except for the whole *look like crap* part. I know you're right. Just...haven't been myself lately."

Debbie shut the fridge door, wiping the strands of hair from her lips. Moving closer, she smiled while wrapping an arm around Merry's shoulder. "You aren't expected to be, sweetie. You've been an emotional zombie for months now, but you're stronger than anyone I've ever met. That's for sure. You've always been the caretaker, not the caretaker-ee, or whatever you

14

want to call it. You know what I mean. It's time to let me back into your world. I know you don't like the idea of leaning on others for some strange reason, but that won't stop me from shoveling healthy food into your face. You need some curves back!"

"My partner thinks Merry's hot. He told me he likes her curves exactly how they are, so leave her alone or you'll have to answer to him."

Merry and Debbie turned to the sound of Derek's voice. All six-foot-three of him crowded the doorway as he leaned against the frame. She couldn't help but smile as Derek came to her rescue.

Again.

Her older brother had an uncanny knack for showing up at the right time ever since she could remember.

Good thing he didn't earlier! Then again, I didn't need rescuing. Peppy did.

Merry let a real smile appear for a brief moment. Derek was all the family she had left, except for a few distance cousins scattered around somewhere. Ones she hadn't seen in years and could hardly remember their full names. Her world had been hewn down to just the two of them. Her burly brother had been her rock ever since childhood but went into overdrive the minute the words "I'm sorry, Sis. Joshua's gone" left his trembling lips barely six months ago.

No. Don't even go there.

Merry noticed Debbie's gaze took in every inch of Derek's body. She stifled a laugh. Poor Debbie suffered from an enormous crush on Derek, one which started when they were in the eighth grade and Derek was a senior. When around Derek, Debbie's normally smart-assed demeanor melted, transforming her into a doe-eyed, giggling, and tongue-tied teenager. If Debbie's cheeks filled with any more blood, they would explode all over the kitchen.

"Good morning, Derek. I wasn't expecting you here today. I didn't see any of your cases on the docket," Debbie gushed.

Derek let a lazy grin slide across his lips. Merry swore she saw Debbie's knees go weak. With a coy wink at Debbie, Derek turned and motioned for Merry to follow him out into the hallway. She doubted Debbie noticed his playful demeanor was fake.

Behind Derek's dark blue eyes, Merry saw a look of what—worry? Anger? Both?

Stay calm. You left nothing behind tying back to you. Nothing. No hair. No fibers. There are no cameras anywhere near that alley. You disappeared before anyone saw you. There is zilch to find. You know exactly why he's here. Remember, act surprised, but don't overreact.

Over his shoulder, Derek muttered, "You've got to stop keeping tabs on me, Debbie, or I might just have to arrest you for stalking."

Debbie giggled like a little girl. Merry couldn't stop the eye roll as she followed Derek down the hall toward her office. Once inside, he waited until Merry was in her seat and then shut the door.

It took everything she had to keep her breath steady...even.

Remember to blink, look Derek in the eye, and play the role of dumbfounded sister with gusto.

Instead of sitting down across from her, Derek came around the desk and leaned against it. "You look like Hell."

"Bite me," Merry teased, keeping her voice light.

Normal.

Derek's eyelids narrowed as he peered closer, his gaze intense. "If I didn't know better, I'd say you've been on a two-or-three day bender. Trouble sleeping again, or is your new obsession with working out taking its toll?"

Of course my sharp-eyed brother notices! Now, take the focus off of me. Don't let him start asking probing questions.

"Wow, you'd make a great cop. Oh, wait..."

Derek laughed, but it was short and hollow. The skin around his eyes tightened as he took in a deep breath. "Funny. Listen, I've got something I need to tell you. Something I believe will put some color back in your face. Allow you to sleep at night. Maybe even eat and put some weight on those bony hips. Deb is right, and Mitch is dead wrong—you need food. Carbs and protein to be exact if you plan on continuing to mold your torso to look like that chick from Terminator."

"Okay, okay. I need to eat!" Merry grimaced, holding her hands up in mock desperation. "I get it. Stop stalling and tell me why you're here. Make it snappy. Court starts in ten minutes, and you know how Judge Tompkins feels about tardiness. If you make me late, I'll tell him it's your fault, and he can chew your ass out in open court. You know, because according to you and Deb, I don't seem to have any meat on mine left to spare."

Derek's tone was soft. "I understand taking your anger out by sweating the pain away, but seriously, Sis. You're pushing your body way too hard."

"You stopped by to see me just to complain about my physique? Exactly how will that help me sleep at night?"

"No, but couldn't stop myself from commenting about your appearance. It's sort of obvious."

Merry pointed to her watch, tapping the glass.

Derek let out a huff of air before asking, "By chance, did you hear about the body found in the alley off 4th Street?"

Blink. Breathe. Play dumb.

"Of course I did. I still watch the news you know. What does that have to do with me?"

"It was Peppy Ramirez."

"What?"

"Someone rolled him. Beat him up pretty bad, and then broke his neck. According to the coroner, he was so full of heroin he probably didn't feel a thing."

Merry figured he expected her to tear up at the news. Let the relief at the knowledge her son's drug dealer was dead run down her cheeks. She knew tears were the appropriate response, yet they refused to appear. Images, smells, sounds, from less than six hours ago filled her mind and senses.

They made her want to grin, not cry. "Oh, shit...not sure what to say or feel."

Derek leaned closer, his arms open wide. Grateful to shield her face from his probing stare, Merry stood. She let him hold her and offer comfort. For a moment, she wished the warmth of the familial connection could soften her heart.

No, you don't. You can't. You already know how things end. How this will destroy Derek when he finds out what you've been up to at night. Remain distant.

"Don't say a word, or even think about it the rest of the day. I told you because you didn't need to hear about it from anyone else. I almost called you earlier but figured I'd let you sleep. Those bags under your eyes tell me I wouldn't have woken you up." Derek patted her back four times, just like their dad used to. "Go, do your job, then come to my house for dinner. I'll cook; you'll eat. Then you can vent. Okay?"

"Thank you for telling me, Derek," Merry mumbled into his shoulder. She had to force the grin on her lips not to seep into the words. Glancing at her watch, she pulled away. "I've...gotta go. See you tonight. Should make it around six, okay?"

Jaw tight, Derek pulled away from the hug. "My baby sister. Tough as aged leather but sweeter than apple pie."

Derek adjusted the gun on his hip as he rose. The familiar sound of the stiff leather brought back memories of their father. Merry didn't say another word. They left her office in silence, each heading in opposite directions. As Merry entered the courtroom, she looked down at her hands, surprised to find they were steady.

Well, it seems my hands are still willing.

3

Finishing the last remaining hearing notification, Merry e-filed it with the clerk's office, and then emailed it out to all counsel. She could hear Judge Tompkins and Debbie talking in the hallway. Pausing to listen, she realized they were standing still. They muttered about the packed courtroom and how tired they both were, plus how thankful they were it was Friday. The Judge groused about having to fill in for a vacationing Judge Rayburn and grumbled about how he was sick of dealing with plea and arraignment rather than the "meatier" cases. Merry grimaced.

Like it really matters!

It was time to tune them out. There was a pressing item to be completed before she left for the day. On the piece of blank paper in front of her, she copied the information from the scanned form on the screen.

De'Shawn Majors, a.k.a. "Mookie"; 139 8th Street, Little Rock; Charges: Contributing to the Delinquency of a Minor; Possession of Narcotics with Intent to Deliver; Possession of Drug Paraphernalia;

Arrest location: 148 8th Street; Arresting Officer: D. Shannon, Badge 4390; U.N.O. ID: Unit 4; Bond: $5,000; Vehicle: none; Gang affiliation: Southern Folks; Tattoos: 6-dice on upper right shoulder and red pitch fork covering back; Trial date – August 15th

She finished by scribbling the remainder of pertinent information down. After seeing Derek's unit was the group of undercover narcotics officers assigned to Mookie, she winced. It meant the possibility was high that, after she dispatched Mookie, Mitch and Derek might end up being part of the investigative team into his death. She didn't see their names listed in the report, and of course, didn't expect to. Undercover cops were only referred to as numbers, and never listed on arrest reports.

Stuffing the paper inside her bag, Merry logged off the computer and shut everything down for the weekend. It was time to head to Derek's and do some sleuthing. The strange twist with Mitch and Derek was a stumbling block, but not one she couldn't overcome. It just meant she would need to take stronger precautions before she killed and make sure to miss nothing and leave no trace behind linking back to her doorstep.

Merry forced herself not to smile while locking her office door. After the stroke of blind luck earlier, she concluded the heavens above must be on her side. Apparently, Maniacal Merry had found favor with the gods of justice. When she saw De'Shawn's name on the docket list Debbie prepared, it was all she could do not to break out into eerie, demented cackles in front of the entire courtroom.

She didn't.

Instead, she grinned.

Like the Cheshire Cat.

Mr. De'Shawn "Mookie" Majors was next in line on her hit list. She already had his number from Peppy's cell phone. She knew De'Shawn was another filthy rung in the long ladder that ended Joshua's life. During her recon missions watching Peppy, she'd witnessed the sack of shit buying his product from Mookie. Plus, she read the text messages exchanged between the two while sitting at the kitchen table earlier. Though veiled with street lingo and slang, she understood enough from years of being around it. A shipment was coming soon. So, when she compared the number Mookie listed on his arrest paperwork with what was stored in the phone she'd copied from Peppy's, it was a match.

Hey, guess what Mookie? I just saved you a ton of legal and court fees! You'll never make your next court date. And your little appearance today saved me lots of recon time. Thanks!

"Merry? A moment please?"

Biting her lip to keep from cussing out loud, Merry cleared her throat. She'd hoped to leave without Judge Tompkins cornering her but figured her luck wouldn't stretch that far. Sure enough, it didn't. She caught a glimpse of Debbie ahead, who motioned she would meet her outside before exiting through the front doors.

Turning around, Merry responded, "Sure thing, Judge. Do I need to grab paper and pen?"

Judge Ronald Arthur Tompkins was right behind her, his enormous brown eyes full of sympathy and concern. Though he usually tried to keep their daily interactions professional, Merry felt there were times they veered into personal territory. After all, before he was Judge Tompkins, he was simply Officer Tompkins, and her father's partner for years.

A thin sheen of sweat glistened off his bald head, his face a pasty gray color. Bushy, white eyebrows, some of the hairs long enough to reach his eyeballs, made her cringe.

What, does the man not have a mirror at home? And why do bald men grow copious amounts of hair on their eyebrows and ears?

She had to look away before the urge to rip them out overtook her.

Merry wondered if he knew about Peppy.

Shit! He'll want to blabber on for hours.

"No need. This isn't about work. It's about you."

"About me, sir?" Merry countered, moving away from her office door. Without the judge even realizing it, he followed her as she took tentative steps toward the front door.

Judge Tompkins put his hand on her arm.

Merry stiffened and stopped. She sensed what was coming next and didn't want to hear it.

"Merry, I'm worried about you."

Yep, there it is! Damn! I don't need sympathy. Or a replacement Daddy figure. I need to go home and start planning, and this stupid conversation is holding me up!

"There's no..."

Judge Tompkins interrupted. "The entire group here in Sixth Division is. Not to mention Debbie and Derek. Especially Derek. He came to see me in chambers earlier. Told me about what happened to Mr. Ramirez. Said he was concerned about how the impact of his death might affect you. He feels—no, we all feel—it might be the straw that breaks the camel's back, so to speak."

"I'm sorry, but what do you mean by that, sir?"

"You have kept all your turmoil bottled up inside, and the consensus is this might be the release valve. What will allow you to experience the pain of losing your family," Judge Tompkins voice trailed off.

A slight twinge of irritation shot up Merry's back. She was over forty years old and Derek still treated her like she was the frightened ten-year-old, terrified of being alone after their mother passed away.

Big brother swoops in to save lil' sis.

"I'm fine, sir. I'll admit, the news does bring a host of mixed feelings, but I'll work through them. My personal life won't affect my performance here, I promise. It certainly hasn't so far, right?"

"No, it has not, but that can and will change if you don't take a break. Everyone has a stress limit. Everyone. Though we admire your determination to stay busy and focus on work, we believe your decision not to take any personal time off was a mistake. You need a chance to heal, to grieve, for your losses."

"Sir, I appreciate that, but..."

Judge Tompkins held up a hand. "The subject is not open for debate. According to H.R., you have over two months of unused PTO. Debbie assures me she can handle your duties while you're out. You'll have your hands full anyway with the move."

"Judge Tompkins…"

"You've worked for me long enough to know when my mind is made up, it can't be changed. Enjoy your time off, Merry. Take care of yourself. Get settled into your new place; travel; take up yoga. Do whatever your heart desires—needs—to get through this. You have my word your job will be here upon your return."

With a fatherly pat on Merry's arm, Judge Tompkins gave her a feeble smile. His bushy brows wriggling, he turned and walked away.

Dumbfounded, Merry simply stared at his black robe fluttering behind him until he disappeared around the corner.

This day can't get any weirder—or better. Maybe I'm really at home, dreaming, because this is just too good to be true!

***

It only took her a few minutes to make it to her car in the parking lot. Debbie leaned against the trunk, her eyes hidden by big, black sunglasses.

Act irritated, not happy!

"If I didn't trust you, I'd swear you just stabbed me in the back to get my job." Merry glared at her friend and unlocked the car door.

Debbie unfurled her arms and yanked off her shades. "Now there you go! A spark of emotion! See? Time away from this hellhole is just what you need, and you haven't even left the parking lot yet! Imagine how much better you'll feel after just twenty-four hours! What you needed was a chance to release all your pent-up feelings before they start leaking out your ears. Don't worry about thanking me. Having your back is what friends are for."

"I don't recall thanking you for butting your nose into my life." Merry yanked the car door open.

Grinning, Debbie reached over and grabbed Merry around the shoulders, forcing a bear hug. "Honey, my nose has been stuck in your business since first grade, or don't you remember?

You may be irritated now, but I have full confidence you won't be later. You know, once you..."

"If you say eat, I'm going to pop you in the jaw. Wipe that smirk of satisfaction right off your face."

Debbie planted a loud, wet kiss on Merry's cheek. "Go. You're going to be late for dinner with Derek. And if you would like to know what I want as a thank you, it's a chance to make his eyes roll back in his head. I've been a happily divorced woman for a whole year now, so he needs to step up to the plate! Just one night with me, and he'll forget every other woman on the planet. That's a promise. I like to think that's why he's never married. He's been secretly waiting for me to be single again."

Merry responded with a snide smile. "No way. You want him, you go after him. Unlike you, I don't meddle in the lives of others. Although after what you two did today, it would serve each of you right to hook up. Both of you are nuts."

"Bye, sweetie. See you next Saturday," Debbie replied, turning on her heels toward her car. "Make sure to tell that hunky brother of yours I'm into guys with handcuffs, so after we finish helping you move, he can take me as his prisoner."

Merry flipped her crazy best friend the bird as she climbed inside the vehicle. She watched Debbie peel out of the parking lot and waited until she was over a block away before a smile appeared. It had taken all of her strength not to let her real emotions free in front of Debbie. What she really wanted to do was hug her right back and jump up and down for joy. Merry wanted to let her laughter loose at the excitement of having sixty days to do nothing but take out every piece of street trash she could.

Merry backed out of the parking lot and cast a woeful glance at the historic Pulaski County Courthouse. The beautiful building stood in silence as she stared at the brick exterior. The dome at the center, covered in stained-glass windows, sparkled underneath the late afternoon sun. Memories of the first time she climbed the sprawling concrete steps, small hand clasped in the huge one of her father, appeared. How mesmerized she'd been, surrounded by marble, porticos, and floors buffed to perfection. The feelings of pride and love as everyone acknowledged them while they walked by, her father dressed in a freshly-pressed uniform.

"Good morning, Officer Clarke. My, what a lovely little partner you have today!" they'd said, grinning.

Those memories are the ones she would miss. Along with the one of her aging father, in a wheelchair and glasses thicker than a bottle of soda, while Derek was sworn in as a Little Rock police officer. Or the lovely reception when she was hired as case coordinator for Judge Tompkins.

The idyllic images seemed two lifetimes ago. They were overshadowed by all the times she heard Joshua's name called, watched him struggle to stand in his orange jumpsuit, hands shackled. Three times she endured sitting in the galley, beyond ashamed as her son stood before the judge for yet another drug arrest. The only solace she could find was the fact Joshua wasn't caught dealing the trash, only buying. Condolences were whispered from other employees or judges, offering words of encouragement and advice.

"Stay strong, Merry. Tough love it what Joshua needs" or "Get him into rehab before it's too late, whether he wants to go or not" or even "Just let him sit in jail for a while. Get Judge Tompkins to pull some strings, keep him locked up. That'll straighten the boy out. Scare him sober."

The one that made her cringe the most was this: "It's not your fault, Merry. Some kids just turn out bad. You and Harold raised him right. Don't blame yourselves."

When Merry made the decision to take matters into her own hands, she knew this day would come. The day her feet trod through the hallowed halls for the final time, she'd assumed would happen because she'd been caught or died. Certainly not from being handed a sixty-day furlough from work to go on a killing spree! The thought made her burst out laughing.

Two full months to learn how to turn murder into art! Yes, the gods of justice have found favor with me. No doubts now.

4

5:30 P.M. FRIDAY AFTERNOON

A bitter smiled tugged at Merry's lips. She pulled up and parked next to Derek's undeniable redneck truck. Bright, Razorback-red with a big Hog sticker on the back window, mud tires so huge they looked like they would crush a horse, and silver, dual exhaust pipes. The only thing it was missing to ensure everyone who saw it knew a Southern boy was behind the wheel was a rebel flag.

Tendrils of smoke from the grill in the backyard floated above and beyond the roofline. She could hear the shrill yaps of Derek's dog, Stonewall. Following the noise and the smells, Merry took off her shoes and padded across the cool stones leading to the back gate. The memories of a hot day last summer when she, Joshua, and Derek worked in tandem to place them flashed by, making her heart skip a beat. Though the heat had been unbearable, it didn't matter. Merry would have tromped through the desert dressed in a parka to work alongside a sober child.

Oh, Joshua. You were clean for eight months! Why in the world did you slip and start using again?

Merry shook the thought away before mind-numbing anger took control. When her hand reached the handle, the wooden door swung open. Stonewall's yips grew louder while he jumped around her feet. She bent down and scooped up the ball of black fluff.

"Oh, you're so terrifying, you big, bad dog." She nuzzled her head with the little Pomeranian's. Stonewall responded by showering her cheeks with wet kisses.

"Stonewall—no licking," Derek said, shutting the gate. He handed Merry a cold glass of tea.

"Says the man who bought a dog that should be calling a twelve-year-old girl his master." Merry set Stonewall down and took a long gulp of tea while surveying the nice spread Derek set out. "Thanks for the drink. Lord, its miserable tonight, and you want to eat outside? After cooking over a fire? That's my brother—crazier than a loon. Smart people cook and eat inside when the temperature and the humidity are near one-hundred degrees. Super intelligent folks order out."

Derek snorted. "Wimp. Try being out in this wearing Kevlar and about twenty pounds of equipment. All night!"

Merry pushed past him, her mouth clamped shut. In the back of her throat, the words, *"Oh, I've put in my share of street time covered in head-to-toe black. Wimp my ass!"* pushed on her vocal chords screaming to come out. Instead, she wandered over to the covered patio, flopping down on the couch. Two large fans whizzed overhead, succeeding in only pushing the hot air around faster.

She took another long swallow of tea while watching Derek putter around with the mountain of food on the grill. Some sort of delicious looking dip with homemade pita chips beckoned from the patio table. Merry's sporadic appetite roared back while staring at the creamy dish. She gobbled down two chips covered in dip. Stonewall came over for a taste. She obliged the little cutie like she always did. Stonewall took the chip and made a beeline for the doggie door.

Even the dog knows it's too hot to eat outside!

From her perch, dinner looked and smelled out-of-this-world. Out of the two of them, Derek was a better cook. When it came to grilling steak, no one was better. Unfortunately, he knew it and loved to rub it in on occasion.

Got to keep my game face on. What would the old Merry say in this situation? Ah, yes, something snarky. Hmm, sort of like the new Merry, just watered down a tad.

"If your cell wasn't on your hip, I'da already pushed your sorry ass into the pool." She knew Derek was waiting for her to say something about his conversation with Judge Tompkins.

"Over a simple comment about being wimpy?"

"Yeah, and the fact you way overstepped the bounds of family duties today. You know, the invisible line most people don't cross out of respect for their loved ones? The line that reads: stay the Hell out of my personal life?"

Derek poked at a slab of meat before turning it. "Inviting my sister to dinner...?"

"Oh, stop the games, will you? You and my supposed best friend stomped all over the line today. If you two were truly so concerned about my wellbeing, you should have talked to me. Not my boss. Do you have any idea how embarrassed I was when he cornered me outside my office? The man basically told me I was a wreck and needed a vacation before I snapped."

Derek faced her, his eyebrows arched in fake confusion. A hint of mischief and concern made his blue eyes sparkle. "I'm sure those aren't the words the Honorable Judge Tompkins used. He's a P.C. kind of guy."

"You know what I mean. Stop acting like this is a joke, Derek. I'm serious here. What you two did to me was wrong, regardless of the reasons for butting into my business."

"You're mad at me because I'm worried about you? Who's the crazy loon now? I'm the big brother which means it's my job to watch over you. Since all this happened, you've become, well, not sure how to put it. Repressed is the word that comes to mind."

"Derek, it's not like I don't appreciate the sentiment behind the gesture. I get it. Really." Merry rose and headed to the jug of tea at the end of the table. After refilling her glass, she continued. "Though I hate admitting it, I know you all are right. I do need time off to deal with..." Merry waved her hand in a dramatic circle, "...My new reality. I'm just saying I would have preferred the topic broached with me first. If you and Deb would have tag-teamed me, you know I would have caved. Then I would have been the one to discuss time off with my boss. Not you."

"That's a load of shit, Sis." Derek closed the lid on the grill and ambled across the patio. In a flash, he was right next to Merry. "We did try to talk you—get you to open up—several times. Each time, we crashed in a ball of flames. If I recall correctly, you told us to mind our own business. So, we watched you continue to stumble along, wilting away little by little each day. Deb and I decided to intervene before your body or mind collapsed because we love you. End of story."

Merry sighed, deciding to let him off the hook. It was difficult to act angry when really, she was beyond ecstatic about her upcoming hiatus from work. It took a lot of internal control to keep from leaping out of the chair while muttering some stupid excuse to go home. More than anything, she wanted to start planning the death of Mookie.

Knowing she would eventually leave the daily lives of her brother and best friend, she decided to spark a flame of interest. One which would hopefully ignite when she was no longer around. "Speaking of Deb, if you don't hurry up and ask her out, she's going to explode. In more ways than one. She's been unhitched for almost a year now."

Derek threw his head back and laughed. "Too bad for her because it's not going to happen. Ever."

Intrigued, and since talking about Deb's infatuation with him wasn't a normal topic of discussion, Merry asked, "Why? I mean, what is it about her you don't like? Her curly, naturally blonde hair? Vivacious personality? Curves that rival Beyonce's? The fact she drools over you and practically worships—no, wait, she does worship—the ground you walk on? Though I certainly don't know why. You're an ass, which is why you've never married. No one could put up with your crap."

Derek shook his head and walked back to the grill. In a

few swift moves, the sizzling steaks were on a plate, followed by a mound of steaming vegetables. "She's not my type, and I've remained unshackled because the thought of having to answer for my every move makes me want to throw up."

"Since when is someone like Deb not every man's type? Oh, wait, I know what you mean. She has a brain! I forget you prefer your women to be dumber than a box of rocks. The collective IQs of the last five you've dated would be hard-pressed to equal their combined cup sizes."

"Nice, Sis. Real nice."

Merry took another sip of tea and watched Derek flip a steak onto her plate. "Truth hurts, huh?"

"If it were the truth, then yes, it would. But it's not. There's no way I'm ever going to ask Debbie Rutherford on a date. Not only is she like another sister, but she's your best friend. Believe me, I've weighed the pros and cons of asking her out before she got married. Even a bit after her divorce. She's a perfect combination of gorgeous, funny, and smart. Don't think I haven't noticed. But the thought of you two discussing our relationship—ugh, no way. The creepy factor is way too high."

"Fair enough." Merry doused her plate with steak sauce and dug in, surprised by her ravenous hunger. The meat was superb. "Glad to know your taste in women isn't as shallow as I've always assumed."

"Will you please stop stalling and talking about meaningless drivel? You're sidestepping real issues that need discussing."

Now there is the cop I know and love. Bam! Right to the point—just like Dad.

"You bitch about my weight, yet while I'm eating, want to talk about things that will make my appetite vanish? Smart move, Detective."

Derek waved his fork in her direction. "Hush. Eat. When we finish, we'll talk. For real with no bullshit."

Rather than argue with him, Merry focused on the delicious dinner.

Yes, we'll talk and all the while, I'll be pumping you for information.

"No. You sit and relax. I'll clean up. That's one of the perks of eating dinner at someone else's." Derek pointed to the living room then loaded the sink with piles of dishes. Without arguing, Merry found a comfortable spot on the cracked leather couch, Stonewall right beside her. Her stomach was packed and she'd finally cooled down. Lack of sleep, a full belly, and a furry companion snuggled against her leg made her a tad drowsy. If left alone for more than five minutes, she'd be out and probably sleep for twenty-four hours straight.

Closing her eyes, she pinched her fingers at the bridge of her nose, hoping to release some of the pent-up pressure in her head. Merry took a long, cleansing breath. Faint wisps of familiar odors tickled her nose.

Mom's hand lotion. Dad's Old Spice. Leather shoe polish. Cinnamon and apples.

She knew it was physically impossible, since it had been twelve years since their father passed and over thirty since Mom died. In her heart, Merry knew it was just wishful thinking that the scents from childhood still remained. The aromas made a small lump in her throat form. Opening her eyes, she downed a large swig of tea to wash it away.

Just like at my house. The only difference is Joshua and Harold's scents are fresher. Yet another reason I put the house on the market.

"I saw that."

"Saw what?" Merry watched Derek cross the living room floor and make his way to the other end of the couch.

"The pain you've kept bottled up so long."

Derek's gaze bored a hole into her soul. Merry knew she would really have to dig deep to extract the information she needed from him without letting her real emotions out. "Better in than out, right?"

"You have that backward. Now, talk to me, Merry. I mean really talk. No bullshit. Let it out, whatever's on your mind. You've been inside your grief shell far too long."

Keeping herself in check, Merry responded. "First, tell me

about Peppy. I want to know everything about how the piece of shit who introduced Joshua to the life, died. It will...take some of the sadness away, I believe. I hope. Make me less prone to kicking the shit out of a punching bag."

For a full thirty seconds, Derek didn't respond. His gaze swept over every inch of Merry's face. What he was looking for, she had no clue. "Fair enough. I believe you've more than earned the right to hear the gory—and confidential—details. Guess having an insider's perspective and insight is a good thing, huh?"

Merry nodded.

"I'm sure I don't need to reiterate the need for..."

"Of course not. I'm well aware you're risking a lot by telling me. It's more than appreciated and my lips are sealed. Spill."

Derek took in a deep breath, held it for several seconds, and then released it in a giant *whoosh*. "A little after three a.m., Peppy received a call from one of his regulars. A pro named Sugar Pie. They agreed to meet in the alleyway off 4th Street. According to Sugar Pie, she planned on working off the price of the smack. Seems Peppy decided to be rolling high when she arrived, but in the dark, must have misjudged the amount he injected. Made him an easy target for anyone lurking about. He was so out of it, he didn't have any defensive wounds. He was too fucked up when someone jumped him from behind. The attack was vicious and quick. However, I think it's doubtful this was just some random robbery that ended in murder."

Yes, it was quick and so not random.

Merry forced herself not to laugh. "Why do you say that?"

Derek took a sip of water before responding. "No drugs were found at the scene, only paraphernalia, which leads to the assumption of a robbery. Of course, it could also be that Sugar Pie helped herself to Peppy's stash before she called us. I really don't believe that's it, either. I watched her interview tape. She was too upset and had a bad case of the shakes, and not just from finding her dealer face-down in a pile of blood. Plus, he wasn't just knocked unconscious and rolled. Someone whipped his ass, up close and personal. His face was a mess. It took an individual with a lot of anger to inflict that much damage."

"Oh, yikes," Merry whispered. To help calm her nerves, she ran her hand over Stonewall's soft fur.

"There's no telling who the fool pissed off over the years. You know, some thug still holding a grudge against the little twerp. When he was my C.I., he was always complaining about someone; there was always a beef between him and at least one other person. Then again, it could be a simple case of being in the wrong place at the wrong time. Another sad sack flying high happens upon him, takes the opportunity to score some fast drugs and quick cash. Again, that scenario is doubtful. I was leaning toward a rival gang, just like the lead on the case. Peppy wasn't exactly the quiet and shy type. He liked to run his mouth, especially in front of other dealers. You know, standard gang posturing and shit. The consensus at the station is another banger got him since they found the symbol for the Street Urchins scrawled in blood next to his body."

Merry honed in on one particular sentence. "You said *was leaning toward*. If his death wasn't gang related, what do you think happened?"

"Mind you, I haven't been to the scene. Captain won't let me or Mitch because, well, of our past connection. What I'm telling you came from John Hudson, the lead on the case. He showed me the pictures, told me the scoop. Said forensics found jack squat at the scene. They found several footprints, but matching them, or even trying to distinguish which one belonged to the killer would be impossible. It's an alleyway, for God's sake. No telling how many people tromp through it each day. But that's all they've got—a huge assortment of shoe treads. Not one hair, fiber, blood spatter, or droplet of sweat. Of course, there are no surveillance cameras in that area, so no video footage to review. You know, it's just ridiculous. God knows our department has been begging the city to install some. It's the most crime-ridden part of town!"

Derek was veering off into his preferred topic for a soapbox rant, so Merry steered him back. "Derek—focus, please?"

"Oh, sorry. Pet peeve."

"Yes, I know. You've discussed it many times before. So, it sounds like Hudson and his team will be hunting for the proverbial needle in a haystack on this one. Hard to believe no trace evidence at all remained."

"Right? Nope, nothing. Which again, leads me to the conclusion I mentioned before—this was a hit. Sugar Pie swore she didn't hear or see a thing. All that leads me to believe Peppy's death was targeted and performed by a pro who wanted to make it look like the death was gang-related. Throw us off track. Hell, who knows? Maybe it's someone who wants to spark a gang war, hoping maybe they'll all turn on each other and kill each other off."

Oh, what a compliment! First kill and already considered a pro!

Derek paused, waiting for a reaction. Her legs were curled underneath her, so she let her left hand rest near her calf, away from Derek's line of vision. She rubbed her face with her other hand, biting the inside of her cheek hard. Tears appeared. She blinked letting a few flow down her face.

Merry wiped her cheek. "As I said before, I'm not sure how this news makes me feel. Right now, the best description would be a weird mixture of satisfaction and shock. I mean, it's sort of like ripping a scab off a wound, you know?"

"Believe me, I know. For me, it's relief."

Confused, Merry queried, "Relief?"

The grin on Derek's face was eerie. When he let his guard down, he was the spitting image of Joshua. He leaned closer, and Merry saw a shimmer of tears behind his eyes.

"Relief I wasn't the one who killed Peppy. It's been a daily struggle for months now, fighting the temptation to wring his scrawny neck. If I just would have arrived sooner that night..."

Stunned by his raw emotion, Merry had to swallow a few times before her tongue unlocked. "Derek...don't. You can't think like that. None of what happened is your fault."

In a huff, Derek stood and began pacing. "Really? Peppy was my C.I. Our meeting that night was going to score the department some great intel about a huge shipment of heroin from Memphis."

Merry pushed Stonewall off her lap and stood. She hated seeing Derek so worked up over something out of his control.

They'd talked about this before, right after Joshua's death, but back then, both she and Derek had been numbed by the events. Time had given them both a chance to soak things up. Remembering. Recalling. All the things each could have done differently if given the opportunity to turn back the clock.

His back was to her and Merry sensed Derek fought back tears. "Wrong. The intel led to a bust stopping hundreds of pounds of that white poison from hitting the streets. You did your job, Derek. How were you supposed to know Joshua slipped and starting using again? Or that Peppy was supplying him again? I mean, you beat the boy up pretty bad when you found out he was Joshua's dealer. Scared the shit out of him, if I recall. And you didn't know it was Joshua who dipped out and ran away when you showed up to your meeting with Peppy. Not until later. So please, stop this."

The anguish on Derek's face made Merry's chest clench with sadness for her brother. She decided to try and inject a bit of humor to change the mood in the air. "Hey? I thought tonight was supposed to be about letting me fall apart, not the other way around. Remember?" Merry's pathetic attempt at humor flopped. When she put her hand on Derek's shoulder, he shrugged it off.

"I know, and I'm sorry. But this news—it brought so many things back to the surface. Made me remember. When I found Joshua…I just, oh, God. I hated myself…because I knew I had to be the one to tell you. Had to break your heart. Look you in the eye and admit I couldn't keep my own nephew safe. Once I saw your face, it was all too real. God, Merry. I'm so sorry."

When Merry reached out to him again, Derek didn't pull away. They clung to each other in their childhood home, weeping as though the world just ended.

For them, it had.

Don't worry, brother. I'm doing what you can't. What your sense of duty and honor forbids you from attempting. What the system won't. I'm making things right. Dad would be so proud of you. He raised a good cop and a wonderful son.

The price for that was he also raised a lethal killer.

5

1:00 P.M. SATURDAY AFTERNOON

She woke up to the sound of whining. When Merry opened her bleary eyes, Stonewall was inches away from her nose. His furry black tail thumped on the couch. She was grateful to be awake, for the recurring dream of the last time she bailed Joshua out of jail, and the wicked fight that ensued, had made her stomach sour.

Noticing the living room was awash in bright, afternoon sun, she pushed up from the couch. Fumbling around for her purse and trying not to step on Stonewall as he ran around in circles.

"Derek?"

Silence.

Yanking open the bag, she pulled out her cell, noticing as she scrolled through messages and a missed call from Derek it was almost one o'clock. "Why did you let me sleep so...?"

Her question drifted away as she listened to the voicemail from Derek.

"Hey, sleepyhead! Sorry, I had to head into work. I'll be out of pocket the next few days on assignment. There's coffee in the kitchen and a pack of chocolate donuts on the counter. Ha ha, just like Dad used to leave us for, remember? Drop some extra food into Stonewall's auto-feeder before you leave, will you? And, uh, hey, I'm sorry about losing it last night. So much for you leaning on my shoulders. Anyway, enjoy your vacation! I think you should go somewhere sunny, like Florida. You need to tan those toned arms! Bye, Sis. Love you. I'll call when I can."

Scrambling to her feet, Merry wasted no time. She flew to the kitchen. In seconds, she'd fired up the coffeemaker, flung some food into Stonewall's feeder, patted the little darling on the head, and then jetted out the door, coffee sloshing as she went.

She'd already wasted almost half of day one of the free sixty, which miffed her to no end. Right now, at least according to her brother, her actions had gone undetected. Merry knew that could change at any moment.

Firing up her car, she backed out of Derek's driveway and gunned the engine. She had to get home and get started.

There were things to do, items to plan, and people to hunt. And kill.

While she drove, she couldn't stop the internal replay of the song that was now her mantra. Her first kill gave her the taste—the addiction—for more.

❋ ❋ ❋

Merry wiped her brow then stretched, grinning at her work. She was beyond meticulous when it came to strategizing. She had to be, or she would never make it up the ladder, never reach the top dog. Because that was her goal: taking out all the lower-level thugs first until she made her way to the source.

The last five hours had been spent, hunched over her dining room table, scouring every inch of the map of Little Rock. Bright, pink stickers marked the cameras placed by the City, none of which were anywhere near Mookie's place. She'd placed blue markers at each police substation, and a big, dark red one where her target lived. The gem of a map was from the Little Rock Planning Commission, where Judge Tompkins was a board member. Lifting a copy had been a breeze, for three had been delivered to their office.

And Merry signed for them.

So, as far as Judge Tompkins was concerned, he'd only received two. Merry simply never corrected the assumption.

Mookie lived only a few blocks from where Peppy's life ended. According to the map, the closest street camera was five streets over, starting near Markham. Parking wouldn't be a problem either. She would stash her car where she did last time. Harold's CPA firm didn't have cameras in the back parking lot, and if her car was ever spotted there, it would be easy enough to explain. The lonely widow needed to be close to familiar places. Parked her vehicle and went for a walk, reminiscing about the past while taking a leisurely night jog.

No one would bat an eye, and the one mile run was a breeze to handle.

Adrenaline made her skin prickle. The rush made her antsy, so she stood and paced around the kitchen as she re-read her notes on Mookie. Unlike Peppy, who'd bounced from one dump to the next, afraid if he stayed too long somewhere he'd get caught, Mookie had his own place. Actually, it was his mother's house. Mookie had taken it over after dear old Mom was convicted and sentenced to twenty-five years in prison for—shock of all shocks—drug trafficking.

Awww, a family business.

How quaint.

Mookie was an only child and his arrest report listed him as single, but that didn't mean he lived alone. Before she continued her plans, Merry needed to know for sure, and there was only one way to find out.

Drive-by and dangle some bait!

It only took thirty minutes for her to transform her look. Her long, red hair was plastered to her skull, hidden under a spiky black wig. She tugged on it, pleased when it didn't budge. It would take a really hard yank to remove it.

Merry had on no makeup, a fake barbed wire tattoo on her

arm, skintight leather pants, a brand new pair of black riding boots, and one of Harold's old wife-beater t-shirts. When she looked at her handiwork in the mirror, she laughed out loud. Her newly acquired muscles rippled under the thin shirt.

Hell yeah. Badass! Hmm, wonder if Harold would have liked this look?

The last thing she needed was stashed away under the couch cushion. Extracting the drugs she took from Peppy, she snickered inside the quiet house. Her plan to offer a deal to Mookie was perfect. After his arrest, she knew his stash would be running on fumes from having his stuff confiscated.

He'd be putty in her hands.

There was only one thing dealers loved more than cash or drugs—the chance to snag more of both.

❋ ❋ ❋

She drove around the outskirts of town for an hour, enjoying the strange connection she felt with Joshua. Driving his treasured bike, the one he bought to celebrate the six-month mark of sobriety, made her heart pound with joy. He'd only had the chance to take it out twice, and this was Merry's sixth ride.

Harsh words had been exchanged between father and son, with Merry stuck as mediator, *again*, when Joshua rolled up on the beast. Harold lit into Joshua for such a stupid purchase, how high his insurance would be (Harold—always the accountant) and the danger of simply riding the thing. Merry ended up siding with Harold (which was a rarity) and tried to persuade Joshua the purchase was a mistake, and that if he ever had an accident, he would have zero protection. Joshua stood firm, saying he was no longer participating in behavior that would kill him. He promised to be a conscientious driver. He'd put his arm around both their necks, hugging them tight, saying he'd put them through enough and having to identify his mangled corpse full of road rash was not going to happen.

The irony didn't escape her.

She decided to stop at Sonic while waiting for the final stragglers from rush hour traffic to dissipate. Removing her helmet, she pushed the button and ordered a limeade. In minutes, the car hop appeared and let out a low whistle.

"Wow! What a ride! Yours?"

No, idiot. I'm just watching it for someone else.

"It was...*is*, my son's. He lets me take her out for a spin now and again. I'm telling you, riding this baby makes me feel young. Better than Botox!"

The kid handed Merry her drink, almost dropping it while he ogled the black and silver machine. "Yeah, I bet! Whoa...you have a son old enough to drive this baby? That's cool. So, what is it?"

Merry couldn't stop herself from grinning at the kid. If his eyes got any wider, they'd fall out onto the hot pavement. She understood why Joshua had bought the expensive toy, and it wasn't just from enjoying the rush when atop it. People were drawn to the bike. It was like sitting on a piece of art.

"Honda VFR1200F."

"Sweet! Your son must be an amazing guy because if I owned this baby, ain't no way I'd let anyone drive it. Especially my mom. She'd wreck it."

Setting the limeade in the cup-holder, Merry slid on Joshua's helmet. The kid's comment irked her for some reason, so she said, "Son, you have no idea what your mother is capable of doing. Given the right circumstances, she could do anything. She just might surprise you."

Merry revved the engine and backed out, leaving the bewildered-looking kid coated in the trail of dust from the bike's tires.

※ ※ ※

Twenty minutes later, Merry turned onto Mookie's street, well aware the bike stood out like a sore thumb. She didn't care. People who saw her would assume she was one of the following: some rich kid from Chenal or The Heights, trolling the hood looking for a score; or the police. If ever questioned, they would report a crazy, black-haired chick with a tattoo riding some fancy, loud bike.

A bike with no tags, since she'd removed them at a gas station a few blocks up from her current location.

The fading, orange rays from the sun cast an eerie glow over the area. The dimming light illuminated the crumbling neighborhood. The houses were old, one-story boxes built in the 40s. Cookie-cutter replicas of each other, like the builders back in the day had no vision, no sense of style. Aged sidewalks, cracked from years of neglect, with weeds jutting through the spaces, were empty. Most of the windows on the front of the houses were either boarded up or had bars on them. Chain link fences surrounded the majority of the dilapidated homes, each in various stages of decline. A few of the overgrown, uncared for yards boasted junkers, some so full of rust the original paint color of the cars was impossible to make out.

This area of town wasn't as bad as Little Rock's version of the hood, which was the southwest part of the city, but it wasn't far behind.

As she approached Mookie's place, Merry stiffened. Mookie was outside, yelling, waving something in the air. Merry realized it was a big two-by-four just as he brought it down in front of him. An old, unkempt holly bush about three feet high blocked her view of what he hit, but it didn't matter. She could tell from the howl of pain ringing down the street before she got close enough to see the dog.

Merry's anger roared to life at the sight. It took a few seconds for her to tamp it back down. She pulled over to the shoulder and shut the bike down. Before she had a chance to yank the helmet off, she heard a woman across the street yell, "Mookie! Ya hit that dawg one more time and I'm gonna call it in! I swear I am! Better yet, I'm gonna come over there and let it loose one night while you'se sleepin'! Let him get a few good bites on ya ass. Serve ya right for bein' so mean to him."

"Fuck you, bitch! Don't be tellin' me my business! Mind ya own. This here's *my* dog, and I'll do what I damned well please!"

Merry reached for her father's old nightstick and the bag of drugs from the side pouch, her gaze never leaving the two quarreling neighbors. Though he continued to scream expletive-filled comments at the elderly neighbor—one who stood on the other side of the fence, hands on hips in a stance only a mother can perfect—Mookie hadn't hit the dog again.

Merry glanced up and down the street. No one else seemed to be outside. At least she didn't see anyone. Hell, it was too freaking hot to venture out. In one swift motion, Merry slid the black, wooden baton out. Pressing it against her leg to conceal it, she held the grip tight. In her left hand, she palmed the baggie full of heroin. Deciding not to remove her helmet just yet, Merry squared her shoulders and walked across the street. In seconds, she stood at the corner of the fence.

Mookie and the annoyed neighbor were in a full-out verbal war and never noticed Merry's approach. He'd moved away from the injured dog, over to the edge of the fence. While he screamed at the woman, who did the same right back, Mookie couldn't keep still. He paced like a caged animal, arms flailing about, going on and on about *his* business and *his* dog.

Yeah, he's jonesing for sure.

Merry took her gaze away from the arguing duo and scanned the house. No bars or wood on the windows. No abandoned toys strewn about. No vehicle in the driveway. The front door was wide open, a TV blaring from the sparse living room. A scrawny, half-starved black pit bull lay on the ground near the base of the front porch steps, bleeding from a large gash to his snout. There were other, older scars from similar looking wounds on its head, back and legs. It made a strange noise Merry couldn't quite place. It wasn't a whimper or a growl—more like a hybrid between the two. She expected the dog to be cowering in terror, fearful of its brutal master, who obviously had a rough hand.

It wasn't.

She could tell, even from the distance separating them, the dog was filled with raw, unabashed hatred. It never acknowledged Merry's presence, for its sole focus was on its horrid master. There was nothing behind its eyes that could even be considered pet-like. Mookie's vicious treatment of the animal had returned the dog to its primal state. Its dark brown eyes were trained on Mookie's back. It inched forward in a slow crawl, away from the steps. From Merry's perspective, it seemed the dog was attempting to sneak up behind Mookie and attack. Hackles raised and lips curled back over its long, yellowish fangs, it only made it as far as the thick rope tied to its neck would allow.

While staring at the poor creature, Merry decided to alter her original plans for Mookie. Under the helmet, a wicked grin lit up her face.

"Yo, dude! What you want? Better be good, or you'll be sorry yo ass came over to this side of the river."

Out of her peripheral vision, Merry could see Mookie to her right, moving with slow, calculated steps. He was less than fifteen feet away, holding the two-by-four like a baseball bat.

Let's get this party started.

Baton still gripped firmly in her right hand, Merry turned. Facing Mookie, she watched his eyes widen when the realization she was female set in. Sliding the visor on the helmet up, Merry let the baggie full of white powder dangle.

Producing her best smile as the bait swayed back and forth, Merry responded, "Mr. Majors, I need someone to help me with a shipment. Peppy mentioned you in a recent conversation. Said you were the best, though I do have my misgivings about his recommendation."

Though still on alert, Merry saw the hunger for the contents of the baggie behind Mookie's eyes. He licked his lips, glanced up and down the street and then back toward the house of his elderly neighbor, who had given up on the argument and retreated inside. Seeing nothing, he tried to keep his tough act up, but Merry heard a twinge of excitement in his voice

"Yeah, I am...which means I don't know what the hell you're talking about, bitch. I don't know anyone by that name. Leave, or I'll feed you to Hercules. I ain't fed him in two days, so you'd be gone in a few bites."

Merry traced Mookie's every move. With slow steps, Mookie made his way to the front porch, careful to keep the distance even between them...and his body out of reach from the dog.

"What, your roommates too afraid to feed him while you were sitting in County, waiting for your turn in front of the judge? You know, from getting pinched after selling to a minor? Perhaps Peppy gave me false information about your skills and I've wasted not only your time, but my own."

Mookie's eyes widened for a second and then narrowed into angry slits. "Ain't got none, and even if I did, Hercules wouldn't eat from...wait, how the hell did you know...?"

"I'm also good at what I do, Mr. Majors. I study the lives of potential business partners with a keen eye. Make sure to pick wisely those I allow into my inner circle. Unfortunately, after Mr. Ramirez's change of plans, I have an opening in my organization and quite a lot of brown sugar in need of distribution."

She watched Mookie clench his jaw, his gaze never leaving the bag in her hand.

"Hmmm, it seems I was given false information from Peppy, so I'll be on my way." Merry turned and only made it three steps before Mookie called out from the porch.

"Wait...how much?"

Pausing in mid-stride, Merry answered. "Enough, Mr. Majors, that just one transaction with me will score us both enough cash to quit the life for good. That is, of course, if you desire to retire at such a young age, as I do. One and done and then a chance to ride off into the sunset. Heat around here is getting too intense for me."

For ten seconds, the only sounds she heard on 8th Street was the humming of traffic from the interstate, the weird grumbles from the dog, and the TV inside Mookie's living room.

"Bring the bike. Park it here, and then come inside. Gotta make sure you ain't wired. Then, we can talk."

With a nod of her head, Merry continued forward until she reached the Honda. Mookie watched her from the front porch while she maneuvered the machine into his driveway. Taking off the helmet, Merry placed it on the seat and then walked up the steps.

"Hold still," Mookie instructed.

He leaned the two-by-four against the doorframe. Merry blocked out the sickening sensation of his hands moving all over her body while he searched for a wire. She had to force the bile back down when he lingered way too long on her breasts and in between her legs. Mookie didn't wait for Merry to offer him a taste of the baggie's contents. Instead, he yanked it from her hand and motioned to the living room. Merry stepped inside and gave the room a quick scan. They were alone, at least in this part of the house.

"Leave that," Mookie said, pointing to the club.

"As I already mentioned, Mr. Majors, I'm very good at what I do. It has kept me from never setting foot inside a police cruiser or jail and free from bullet holes or other injuries. If the club goes, so do I. In this business, one can't be too careful. Don't want to end up like Peppy. Agree?"

The stare-down between the two lasted a full minute. Every muscle in Merry's body was tensed, ready to unleash holy hell if things soured. In the end, she had read Mookie right. The craving for a hit and the chance to score a ton of cash was too much for Mookie to pass up.

"Some attitude ya got, bitch. Fine. Sit. Let's talk while I try a sample. Whatta ya mean 'end up like Peppy'? You sayin' dude's on the slab?"

Yes, let's. Enjoy the interaction because it will be one of the last you ever have in Mommy's house.

Bastard.

"I am. Guess you missed that tidbit of local gossip while in lockup, huh? I'm surprised your handler didn't mention it. If you were my C.I., I'd a already questioned you because of your affiliation with Peppy. Ask you if you decided to take out some competition."

"How...?" Mookie's question trailed off. He bit his lip instead of saying anything else.

Merry graced the lowlife with a sly grin. "My sources, Mr. Majors. Didn't you hear me earlier when I said I make sure to unearth all the information I can on a potential partner?"

Mookie nodded.

"Don't worry about it, though. I guarantee you won't be questioned because my sources informed me the Urchins took him out, which is why I'm shopping for a partner on this side of the town."

"Urchins, huh? Peppy shoulda known better than to piss in their territory. They's meaner than ol' Hercules."

So am I.

Mookie's focus was back on the baggie. Eagerness danced behind his dark brown eyes. A faint hint of what Merry could only guess was his version of a smile tugged at his lips. "Guess Peppy's loss is my gain, huh? Gotta say, I'm surprised he was steppin' out on Tee...I mean, our supplier. Guarantee you that's who took him out. Competition is fierce in this town, and Peppy knew *way* too much. Thug life. Gotta love it."

Bonus intel to extract later!

"Mr. Ramirez's death does not concern me, and I don't think it should you either. After all, we're both still here, right? Means we're smart. Streetwise. Business savvy. I believe we both have a lot to gain by forming a partnership between just the two of us, Mr. Majors. So, go ahead. Indulge. Trust me. I know you'll love what I have to offer. Its killer shit."

6

7:45 P.M. SATURDAY NIGHT

Merry stood by the open door, unwilling to sit anywhere in the cesspool Mookie called home. Plus, she needed to remain on guard, and if necessary, be close to an escape route. Fresh air was also a factor. The place reeked almost as bad as the alleyway dumpster.

Mookie seemed to forget another person—*no, a complete and total stranger*—was in his living room. The fool was too busy fiddling with the baggie. He examined it like he was testing out fine wine. Held it up to the bare light bulb on the lamp beside him, turning the sack round and round. He stuck his nose inside the opening and sniffed, as though it were a fresh flower. The gesture was followed by poking his index finger inside, letting a sliver of white coat it. Mookie rubbed the powder between his thumb and finger and then across his gums.

The scumbag's fascination with the smack gave Merry a brief moment to study her surroundings. No decorations on the dirty, bare walls. A couch crammed in one corner, sporting more holes than material. Empty fast-food containers were scattered on the small coffee table and the floor around it. Ashtrays overflowed with cigarette butts and drug paraphernalia. The living area opened directly into the kitchen, which was a disaster zone. Garbage littered almost the entire linoleum floor. A roach skittered over the toe of her boot.

In stark contrast to the squalor, a large flat-screen TV was mounted on the wall. Expensive looking jeans, t-shirts, and a leather jacket were draped on the one chair pushed up against a card table. A hookah at least four feet tall rested in the other corner.

Lovely priorities.

Merry turned her attention back to Mookie right as he loaded his nose up with a full snort. The sounds coming from him made her stomach roll. Within seconds, Mookie was no longer shaking. She could see his pupils dilate into enormous, black saucers. His shoulders drooped, and he moved almost in slow motion over to the couch. His body melded into the folds the second he flopped down.

"So, what do you think, Mr. Majors? Top grade, right?"

Mookie wiped his nose twice. His eyes closed as he rode the rush. "Straight! Damn straight. Stuff's better than Memphis Yellow we get from…" Mookie clamped his mouth shut, shaking his head. "Where's it from, and why ain't you hitting any?"

Ah, thank you for that little nugget of knowledge. Tee somebody-or-other brings it from Memphis. Good to know.

"Let's just say, the shipment I'm waiting on is actually being shipped. You'll be the one picking it up and driving back. That's all you need to know for now, Mr. Majors. Recall I mentioned I'm good at what I do? That's because I don't' get fucked up when making business deals. I fly high when in the safety of my home."

Mookie blinked so slow, it looked like his eyelids weighed thirty pounds. It took him a few seconds to gather his thoughts and form words. "What's your name, and tell me again how you know so much about me? I ain't never seen you before. You ain't wired and ain't sampling. I swear I smell cop."

Merry laughed. "You still stuck on that, Mookie? I assure

you, I'm not associated in any way with law enforcement, though I do have plenty of connections at the department. Why do you think I've stayed out of trouble for so long? I believe you and I have the same handler. I just...give him certain favors to remain un-cuffed."

A lazy grin spread across Mookie's slack jaw. "Yeah, you look like his type. He likes them lean and mean."

Damn! Mitch must be his handler.

"Oh, and my name's Ms. Nyical. That's all you're getting today. So, Mr. Majors, do you think you'd have any problems selling this to your regulars?"

Mookie laughed, and a dribble of saliva inched out of the corner of his mouth. "Hell no. Might even bring me some new hitters once word gets out."

"Perfect! I'll see you at three a.m. on Monday morning. Alleyway between 4th and 5th. Come alone and ready to take a drive, Mr. Majors. Oh, and please bring something better than your stick of wood over there for protection." Merry nodded toward the two-by-four. "Because the boys we'll be meeting make the Urchins look like Boy Scouts."

It took two attempts for Mookie to stand. He wobbled across the floor, stopping directly in front of Merry. Eyelids hooded, breath foul, and lips wet, Mookie grabbed Merry's left breast and squeezed. His other arm pinned her wrist holding the club to her side. "What makes you think you're leaving here without me sampling some of you?"

Merry's gaze was near even with the lowlife's. He was maybe an inch or so taller, thin as a rail, yet full of lean muscle. It would be a struggle, but she had every confidence she'd prevail over his drugged-out ass. Her first instinct was to bash his stained teeth in with the club, but that would only complicate matters. It wasn't the right time to take him out.

Instead of liberating his teeth from the filthy hole he called his mouth, Merry jerked her free arm forward, grabbing Mookie's crotch. She applied enough pressure that Mookie groaned, his hands dropping to his sides, smile long gone. "I don't screw my business partners, Mr. Majors. That privilege is reserved for those who keep me out of jail, and men with big

51

cocks." Merry squeezed with all her might and then let go as Mookie fell to his knees. "You don't fall into either of those categories. I'm afraid I'm all out of samples for you. See you in two days—if you can walk."

As Mookie cupped his crushed family jewels, Merry moved past him and snatched the baggie. With a flick of the wrist, she dumped the remaining powder onto the makeshift coffee table. Pocketing the empty baggie, she gave Mookie a sinister grin while stepping over him.

She turned and walked down the steps. Her gaze was focused on the dog, who was less than fifteen feet away. Muzzle still covered in blood, it never made a sound as it watched Merry extract the keys from her pocket.

Don't worry, Hercules. Your chance for revenge is coming.
Soon.

***

Mookie watched the crazy white ho stroll down the front steps. He wanted to get up and knock the bitch into the next week. He couldn't even yell at her because nothing on him functioned at the moment. Though wasted, he'd lost the ability to do much of anything except crumple to the floor and groan. It was too bad she didn't trip and land near Hercules. He would have enjoyed watching Ms. Nyical get gnawed on like a stack of ribs.

His breathing returned to normal just as he heard the *vroom* of the bike from the driveway. Vocal chords finally working, he let out his pain and anger in an explosive outburst.

He crawled to the couch and reached under the cushion for his cell. Eyes still watering, it took him a few seconds to scroll down and find the right number. He hit *send* and waited, rubbing his crushed balls.

"News already for me, De'Shawn?"

Mookie grumbled, "Oh yeah."

"Wow, I'm proud of you boy! Must have decided you didn't like your recent stay with us, huh? Now see there? I just knew you had some information lurking around in that head of yours. Must say I'm surprised you didn't spill it before."

"Fuck you. I held up my end of the bargain when y'all busted me! I didn't say shit! Now, I got some proper info. Wanna hear what I gotta say or not?"

"Such harsh language, De'Shawn! What would your mother say if she heard her precious Mookie..."

"Don't you dare bring Moms into this. You promised if I gave you any information, you'd make sure she's..."

The voice on the other line was a low grumble, making the hairs stand up on Mookie's arms.

"Don't start getting bossy with me, De'Shawn, or your moms might spend some time in solitary. Now, quit wasting my time and talk."

Mookie swallowed his anger and responded, "Got a visit today from some crazy ho. Said she was one of yours."

There was a long pause before a response was given. "Did you now?"

"Yeah. Bitch had her some nice product. Said she needs help with the process. Going down at three a.m. Monday at Peppy's favorite spot. Said it's enough we could both give up the life for good."

"Description, please?"

"White. Tall as me with short, black hair. Had one of them barbed wire tats on her arm. Said her name was Ms. Nyical. Rode up here on some fancy bike. Gave me a sample, and I'm telling you, it's proper."

"Interesting. Anything else you want to share?"

Mookie scooted around until he found a comfortable position on the couch. The burning pain between his legs had dulled to a heavy throb. He stared at the powder all over the table, eager to get after some more. "Told me to come alone. Be ready to take a drive. So whaddya want me to do? Show up, or leave it up to you?"

"You just proceed as instructed. I'll handle things on my end."

Mookie heard the anger in the voice and grimaced. "So, we good on our deal? Moms will be okay, right?"

Mookie's answer was dead air.

7

8:00 P.M. SATURDAY NIGHT

While the sun cast the last rays of light before disappearing over the horizon, Mitchell Sinclair watched the neighbor's cat scurry across his front yard. The orange and white tabby stopped in mid-stride, eyes focused on a bird in the oak tree. The annoying bird chirped away, oblivious to the four-legged predator watching from below. For some reason, Mitchell found the entire spectacle fascinating. It was like having a front row seat at *Animal Planet* or *The Discovery Channel*, all in the comfort of a screened-in porch. Even a domesticated pet, raised by a loving family—its needs, wants, and hunger always met—still retained its instinctive nature to stalk and kill.

He took the final sip of beer and smiled as Clara stepped outside, two beers in hand. Judging by the jiggle of her full breasts, she still wore only his t-shirt from their previous romp in the kitchen, hallway, and eventually, bedroom. He eyed her long, muscular legs as he recalled how they looked when in mid-air.

"Perfect timing. That's why I keep you around."

Clara handed Mitch a can and joined him on the swing. "Wrong. I stay for the free booze and cable."

Mitch leaned over and stuck his hand between Clara's legs. He rubbed hard, enjoying the look of lust spark to life behind Clara's dark brown eyes. They both knew the only reason he continued seeing Clara was they both had an insatiable libido. Her small gasp of surprise excited him. "You stay because I make you cum loud and hard."

Clara let out a groan as Mitch's fingers increased their pressure. "You sure are full of yourself, Detective."

Her voice was low, seductive. Full of raw passion. Mitch let his fingers slide inside. She was beyond ready, and his eagerness grew in response. He nipped her ear and whispered, "I'm not the one who's about to be full of me."

Clara wrapped her fingers around Mitch's blond curls, pushing his lips toward her own. When his strong fingers worked in unison with his talented tongue, Clara's troubles evaporated.

Her chance at mind-numbing ecstasy ended the minute Mitch's cell phone rang.

"Ignore it," Clara pleaded. "Please? I need you—right now!"

Mitch jerked his head and hand away, ignoring the girl's pleas. He stood and retrieved the cell he used only for work from his pocket. He didn't even cast a glance in Clara's direction as he exited into the back yard.

Irritated, Clara sighed as Mitch disappeared into the night. When he got a call from work, his mood shifted so fast, it was like he morphed into someone else. Not that Mitchell Sinclair was anything near a warm, caring human being when off duty, but still, the flip-flop was scary at times. Jekyll and Hyde shit.

Cracking open a beer, Clara muttered, "Another evening shot to hell; a night of humping like rabbits—poof!—gone with just one freaking phone call. Damn good thing I brought my vibrator."

Shifting in the seat, the ache between her thighs still thrumming, Clara sipped the cold beer. She strained her ears to make out what Mitch said, yet heard only the rumble of his voice. He was too far away from her position to make out the words.

Clara was tired of being Mitch's "off-duty booty" as he called it. Their relationship wasn't really a relationship at all. After admiring each other's physiques at the gym almost one-year ago, the magnetic sexual attraction between them hot enough to melt snow, their fuckfests started. Clara sensed the darkness in Mitch lurking just below the surface, and it pulled her inside his web. Like so many other women, Clara naively assumed she could "fix" Mitch's wounded psyche. Given the fact he was a cop, it made sense to her. No telling what kind of horrible things the man had witnessed over the years.

All that changed the night his partner's nephew died.

Mitch withdrew, mentally and physically. No more short bouts of playful post-coitus cuddling. Hot and heavy lovemaking transformed into simply raw, carnal sex. Time together was spent only at Mitch's insistence, not hers. Basically, when Mitch had time off work and a woody, he called. The conversations about moving in together ceased.

Clara swiped a tear from her cheek. Gulping down the rest of the beer, she forced herself not to let a full crying jag start. She couldn't really blame Mitch for everything. She shouldered part of the blame by continuing to participate in an unhealthy relationship.

"No, I'll break through his shields—one day."

"Wrong." Mitch yanked the screen door open and tromped inside.

Clara felt the negative energy fill the room up. She knew before he said a word it was time for her to get dressed and go home.

Mitch grumbled, "Got called in. Don't know how long I'll be."

Without a word, Clara rose and went inside to get dressed, tears of anger and irritation making her vision blur.

Mitch saw the disappointment on Clara's face as she crammed her clothes in the overnight bag. He knew what he was doing to the girl wasn't fair, but damn she was fun to have around. He knew, from numerous other failed attempts, a long-term union with an undercover cop eventually ended. And with all the mess going on in his life now, it was time to cut the cord.

"Stop sulking. I told you in the beginning my job was my number one priority."

Clara jerked the bag onto her shoulder. "I'm not sulking. I'm just...sick of this shit. If I lived here, I..."

"You don't, and you never will. I told you before, I will never marry again. And shacking up is marriage without paper."

Tears burst out of Clara's eyes as her anger boiled. "Screw you, Mitch. I'm done."

Mitch never said a word in response as Clara stormed out of the house. He didn't have the time or interest to dwell on it.

There were other, much more important things to handle besides a clingy woman.

Because the phone conversation minutes ago screwed up everything.

"Fuck!" Mitch screamed as he slammed his fist into the wall.

***

Finished with reattaching the license plate, Merry yanked the itchy wig off. Her scalp felt like it was on fire, so she removed all the bobby pins holding her hair in place. She stuffed all the gear into the side saddle bag. Gunning the engine, she pulled back onto the road from the shoulder. In minutes, she was on the freeway, heading west toward the vibrant orange sky.

It took ten miles of open road for her hands to stop shaking and heart rate to slow down. Rage boiled inside her mind. There wasn't enough water and soap in the world to wipe the filth Mookie's touch left on her skin. It took control she didn't realize she possessed to keep from killing him in broad daylight.

Watching him devour the heroin made her feel sick.

And it made her think about Joshua.

No ruminating in the past!

Shifting her concentration back to the road, Merry thought about the meeting. She found out some great information to delve deeper into later while Mookie was under her control. Forty-eight hours worth of planning to complete before the fake meeting with the lowlife bastard.

The rush of the ride wasn't enough to surpass the pull to finish strategizing. There were a few steps she would need to alter after the discovery of the dog. Her first instinct was to put in an anonymous call to Animal Control. Report not only the abuse, but the violation of the pit bull laws in Little Rock. Get the dog taken away before Mookie hurt it again.

Then, she looked into the eyes of Hercules and realized there was no hope for salvation. The dog didn't stand a chance at rehabilitation. Merry sensed the brokenness, the return to raw predator. She knew what would happen to the dog in the end. No matter which decision she picked, Hercules would be put down as a vicious dog. It would be, after all, the most humane thing to do.

So, instead of calling it in, Merry decided Hercules needed his own revenge before his life ended. Merry would give Hercules a chance for some payback for the untold amount of abuse suffered by the hands of his cruel master.

Lost in thought, she almost missed her exit. She cut across two lanes, thankful the freeway wasn't packed. In minutes, she pulled up the tall, chain link fence surrounding Store-N-Go. Punching in the security code, she waited while the gate slid back. It gave her a chance to survey the area. Thankful no one seemed to be out perusing through their storage units, she drove to her spot.

Once she shut the engine down, she paused to listen for sounds of another vehicle or people talking. Hearing nothing other than the faint hum of traffic on I-30, she unlocked her unit and pushed the bike into its designated spot by the front. She was grateful it was almost dark so she couldn't see all the items stored inside.

Like it really matters! You know what's inside—all the treasures from your old life!

In four quick strides, she was at her car, which was parked at the end of the aisle. Unlocking the trunk, she pulled out a black gym bag and then trotted back to the interior of the

59

storage unit. With one final glance to ensure she was alone, Merry changed clothes. It took her a few attempts to remove the tight leather pants. All the sweat she'd accumulated over the last two hours made them stick to her thighs like they'd been glued on.

She stuffed all her attire, including the black wig, her boots, and the empty baggie, inside the bag. The only thing she couldn't remove, at least not yet, was the fake tattoo on her arm. It would have to wait until she made it home and hit the shower.

Turning to leave, the force of what was near her right, beckoned. She didn't want to, but the pull was too strong to ignore. Steadying herself, Merry looked.

The picture was a 16 x 20 family portrait, taken at The Old Mill in North Little Rock. Even in the darkness, she knew every inch of the picture. It had been taken in late September, just as the trees and shrubs exploded in a burst of reds and yellows. It was still sweltering outside, so they all sported white cotton outfits. Harold and Joshua were in golf shorts and t-shirts, and Merry wore a long, flowing dress. They sat along the edge of the tree-branch-entwined bridge leading to the replica of an old, water-powered grist mill.

Joshua's hair glistened in the setting sun, making sparks of red bounce off his dark curls. Harold looked relaxed and dapper, his once-dark head of hair heavily interspersed with gray. Derek completed the foursome, one hand protectively resting on Joshua's shoulder. When the proofs were viewed, all of them laughed at how much Joshua's features had changed over the years, because he looked more and more like his Uncle Derek.

The picture of their small family was shot only two weeks before Joshua's injury. It was a bitter reminder of how effortless and easy their life had been. How much love, how freaking naïve, they all were while they smiled wide for the camera.

Merry slammed the metal door shut and ran to her car. She flung the gym bag in the passenger seat and shoved the keys into the ignition. While waiting for the gate to open, she bit her lip so hard to keep her tears inside that blood leaked from her mouth and down her shirt.

She gave the gas pedal a hard stomp, and tires squalled. On

autopilot, she drove home in the darkness, using all her anger as fuel for the inferno she was about to unleash on De'Shawn Majors.

8

9:00 P.M. SATURDAY NIGHT

After taking the world's longest shower, Merry wrapped herself in a robe and padded to the kitchen. Though she didn't want to, it was time to look at her cell phone. There was no telling how many calls and texts she'd missed while on her little baiting mission. She was glad she'd shut down her social media accounts and only had her phone to contend with.

Grabbing an energy drink from the near-empty fridge, she snatched her phone off the counter and walked into the sparse living room. It was still strange to see the house so empty. Most of her belongings were squirreled away in the storage unit. Only big items like the couch, kitchen table, china hutch, bedroom furniture, and all of Harold's office furniture, remained.

Merry scrolled through her phone. Seven missed calls, four of them from Debbie. One from Carol Kramer, her real estate agent, one from Harold's former partner, Steve Witherspoon, and another from a number she vaguely recognized. She knew Debbie would want to chat, and honestly, Merry wasn't in the mood. Though she adored her closest friend, she didn't want to spend an hour or more listening to Deb prattle on about mundane, trivial bullshit.

No, that's not true: I do want that. But normalcy isn't part of my serial killer lifestyle anymore, now is it? Besides, I need to start pulling away from not only Deb, but Derek. It will make things easier for them when all this is over. What am I going to tell her when she asks how my day was? She'd flip out if I mentioned my trip to the hood and the handful of balls I crushed.

Carol and Steve both left voicemails, so Merry listened. Carol's chirpy little voice requested a callback "only if you need me" and thanked Merry again for allowing her to be of service "during this incredibly difficult time." Before hanging up, Carol made sure to leave a bit of her own bait by mentioning in a sweet, innocent voice, "Remember, if you need any help finding a new place, just call!"

"Thanks, but I've already accomplished that on my own," Merry muttered into the mouthpiece.

The message from Steve made her heart skip a few beats.

"Merry? It's Steve. How are you? Haven't heard from you in a few weeks, and—you know—I was worried. I know you're probably busy with preparing to move and all, but, I just—oh, I'm sorry. I swear I'm not trying to poke an unwelcomed nose into your life. Really. It's just—okay, I know this is going to sound odd—but, where are you moving to? You haven't mentioned anything about a new place yet, and the folks here at the office want to be able to bring you a housewarming gift. But that's not the only reason I need to talk to you. The, um, insurance company handling our claim for benefits can't seem to locate the copy of Harold's uh, death certificate. I hate to ask, but do you have one more? If not, could you please order another? Let's schedule a time to talk..."

In a fit of rage, Merry screamed as she hurled the phone across the room. The second it crashed into the brick fireplace, it shattered into tiny pieces. She jerked off the robe and headed straight to the laundry basket at the edge of the steps. In seconds, she was dressed in her workout clothes. Her feet pounded down the stairs and into the garage.

She attacked Joshua's old punching bag, not even bothering to put gloves on. Within minutes, the dirty white bag was coated with a thin sheen of red from her bleeding knuckles.

***

Derek shifted his body in the seat. He'd been sitting in the same position so long his butt was numb. The list of things he hated was long, but waiting was definitely in the top five. Unwilling to risk the light from his phone giving his presence away, he gazed out the windshield. The sun was completely gone, so he surmised it was close to nine p.m.

He sighed and cracked his knuckles. Years of undercover work helped elongate his tolerance level to being inside a hot car, but this excursion was different. Derek's mind raced in a hundred directions, and each spur ended up converging at the junction of Merry's woes.

His baby sister—there was no one like the red-headed spitfire. Derek had watched her change numerous times over the years. Before their mother died, Merry had truly been the perfect name. She was full of smiles and had an adorable laugh, her mop of curly red hair flapping around like a superhero cape.

Though he would never tell her, secretly, Derek had been jealous of the attention showered on Merry the minute she arrived in a pink blanket from the hospital. For the first few years, Derek kept his physical and mental distance from her, only connecting with her once she was old enough to tag along on fishing trips. Of course, that had been forced upon him. The first time the subject was brought up, their father pulled Derek aside and informed him Merry was coming. Ten-year-old Derek threw his final, rip-snorting fit. He whined about how he didn't want to share time he considered special between him and his dad with anyone, much less his annoying little sister. His father had yanked him by the arm and took him outside, where he promptly cut down a switch and applied it to Derek's bare legs.

"You will never, ever talk back to me like that again, understand? Merry is your flesh and blood! You're to love her, protect her, and guide her in ways your ma and I can't. 'Cause one day, we ain't gonna be here to take care of her. Got it?"

With tears of pain, shame, and embarrassment racing down his cheeks, Derek nodded. Too humiliated to verbalize a response, the last lick his father ever laid on him came next.

"What's the proper response?"

"Yes...sir," Derek muttered through his tears.

To Derek's surprise, Merry's first fishing trip ended up solidifying their relationship. At least on his end after Merry nearly drowned. When a fish nibbled at the line, the excitement made her jump up in the boat and over she went.

Without a lifejacket and no ability to swim.

At that moment, watching his little sister sputter and thrash in the water, head bouncing up and down like a bobber, something inside Derek's ten-year-old mind snapped. He froze, and watched in terrified awe as his father dove in and snatched a screaming Merry by her shoulder just as her head disappeared below the surface.

Under the influence of his own panic, their father was too rough with Merry as he yanked her out of the water. He pulled too hard and dislocated Merry's shoulder. Confused, frightened, and in pain, Merry scooted away from her father and clung to Derek. Her big blue eyes were full of tears as she whimpered, "Help me, Derek!"

That's all it took for Derek's heart to melt as love for his sister flooded his soul.

The day she almost drowned scarred Merry for years. Made her terrified of water, a fear she never learned to overcome. Gone was the peppy, energetic girl with the huge grin, replaced by a shy introvert. The summer Merry turned ten, she'd emerged from her shy-shell as she grew closer to Debbie, only to re-enter it when their mom died in a car accident.

Until Merry hit her teens, she remained distant. Their father was no help, for the minute their mom died, he turned to work to soothe his broken heart. Derek understood the decision since he was a man, or a reasonable facsimile of one at fifteen.

Merry, on the other hand, did not.

Unsure and certainly unprepared in how to handle the

upheavals in their lives, Derek simply decided to treat Merry like a little brother. He taught her to play football, ride a bike, skateboard, spit, throw a fastball. He tried, and failed, numerous times to teach her to swim. Anything and everything he did, a little red-headed shadow was by his side, absorbing it all.

Then, almost overnight, his shy little buddy disappeared. When Merry hit puberty, a new creature emerged. One who wasn't afraid of anyone or any damned thing. Merry went from riding a Huffy to racing Derek's old dirt bike against the older neighborhood kids. She could throw a football better, farther, and more accurately than any guy at school, including Derek. She pestered their father for months until he caved and paid for karate lessons, then got her black belt in less than a year. She refused to date the nice guys. Merry was drawn to the dudes even Derek wouldn't have hung out with during his own rebellious teenage years.

No, Merry wasn't just rebellious. She had been addicted to danger.

Tomboy through and through, Merry suffered from lack of a maternal hand in upbringing to soften her rough edges. Neither men in her life could help, for each had their own painful secrets and heartache they struggled with.

When he graduated high school and left for college, Merry really rebelled. Got caught smoking, drinking, and dating older men. Dad would yell at her, ground her, but never laid a switch to her backside, which sort of annoyed Derek. At a loss as to how to corral his headstrong daughter, their dad gave up and buried himself even deeper into work.

Thankfully, Merry's rebellious years ended the minute she met Harold Hall. During one of the numerous telephone conversations with his very overwhelmed father, Derek made the suggestion to get Merry into yoga. Many of the girls at college were doing it, and he figured it surely couldn't hurt. It took Derek calling his mouthy sister and threatening to leave Fayetteville and come home to kick her scrawny ass before she submitted and went to her first class.

After the first day, Merry never had to be persuaded again because she fell, hard and heavy, for Harold. Just months after graduating high school, against their father's strenuous objections, they got married.

When Joshua arrived two years later, the defiant teenager was nothing more than a fleeting memory. Though Derek and his dad had never really been too fond of Harold since they were on completely opposite sides of just about every conceivable thing possible, they tolerated him for the transformation of Merry. Harold's calm nature, scientifically-inclined mind, and boring-as-hell consistent demeanor, rubbed off on his previously high-strung sister.

All that began to unravel when Joshua got hooked on drugs. Little by little, the old, angry Merry emerged. When Joshua and Harold died, Merry completely reverted. Derek didn't need confirmation he was correct because he sensed it. Could see the deep, unhinged anger behind her eyes. Recognized it from her youth. There was an edginess to her now, and not just from the grief of losing husband and child. Something sinister bubbled and churned inside her, and it made Derek's heart heavy.

Derek knew it wasn't a question of if, but when, Merry's mind would snap, and he felt helpless to stop it.

All the years he'd spent shielding his sister from things she never needed to know about didn't seem to matter anymore.

The trip down terrible memory lane ended when Derek saw the signal he'd been waiting for. He turned his focus to the task at hand, grateful for the distraction of work.

※ ※ ※

The last ten minutes spread-eagled on the cold, concrete floor, Merry's breathing returned back to normal. When she stood, her sweat-soaked skin made a strange sucking noise. The intense, two-hour workout brought her focus back where it should be...planning.

After bandaging her bloodied knuckles, Merry extracted a new ensemble from the hidden spot she'd stashed her supplies. The three enormous coolers Harold bought for parties by the pool were crammed full. A fresh pair of boots, pants, shirt, vest, and wig in hand, she dashed back inside.

Ignoring the mess she made in the living room earlier, Merry went straight to the junk drawer in the kitchen. Removing the duct tape and scissors, she plopped down in the middle of the floor. It didn't take too long to wrap the souls of the boots with tape. Once finished, she stuffed everything inside the backpack. Scooting across the floor, she opened the bottom cabinet and reached inside. Her father's old hunting knife was the last item she would need.

Staring at the thin, silver blade, Merry decided to hone it to perfection before sliding it inside the bag. A wide smile appeared at the thought of slicing Mookie's balls off then feeding them to Hercules.

"Oh, how very twisted of you!"

Merry's laugh was cynical, bitter, and full of madness.

And she loved it.

Part one of her project completed, it was time to study. She needed to go through Peppy's phone again and start a mental flow chart of all his connections.

Just as she sat down at the kitchen table, the doorbell rang. Glancing at the microwave, she was surprised to see it was almost midnight.

Who the Hell is at my door? Oh, shit. Please don't let it be about Derek! Wait...was I followed?

She leaned over and took the knife out from the backpack. Her bare feet made no noise as she crossed the kitchen floor then padded down the steps. Heart pounding, she flipped on the porch light and peered through the peephole, blade at the ready.

What she saw made her gasp in shock.

Though older, the long, blonde hair and beautiful face was unmistakable.

Savannah?

Merry stood frozen for a few seconds, her mouth hanging agape. She hadn't seen the girl since Joshua's funeral, and it had only been a brief reconnection.

What is she doing here? Wait? Is she? Oh, my GOD!

Stashing the knife in the umbrella stand to her right, Merry opened the door.

"Savannah? What are you doing here so late?"

"Hey, Mrs. Hall. Sorry to stop by so late, but I really need to talk to you. I tried calling you..."

Merry remembered who the mystery number on her phone belonged to now.

"I'm sorry, I've been busy packing. Planned on calling you back tonight, but I, uh, broke my phone."

Obviously nervous, Merry watched Savannah as she rubbed her swollen belly.

For a few seconds, they both stared at each other without uttering a sound. Merry's heart beat so fast she feared it would burst from her chest. Eyeing Savannah's very pregnant belly, Merry finally said, "Please, come inside. Looks like you have something you need to tell me about."

"Yes, ma'am. I sure do." Savannah produced a weak smile and nodded.

Merry held the door wide and let the girl inside, head spinning from lack of sleep, physical exhaustion, and shock. A sprig of hope pounded in her chest.

Is it possible I'm going to be a Grandma?

9

"Would you like something to drink?"

"Water would be great. It's still sweltering outside, and I'm afraid in my condition, the heat really bothers me."

Merry motioned to the couch. "Have a seat. I'll be right back." Forcing her steps to remain normal, Merry grabbed a bottle of water from the fridge. In seconds, she was back in the living room. "Here you go."

Savannah took a tentative sip. "Thanks. Oh my, Mrs. Hall! What happened to your hands?"

"Oh, I'm not very good at...doing certain things around the house myself. It's nothing. Banged up my knuckles while packing."

"You're moving?"

"Yes. Decided it was time to make some changes in my life. Next Saturday will be the last day I spend here."

"That makes me feel a bit better. When I walked in and

saw how empty it was, I thought maybe you'd sold a bunch of stuff—you know—to make ends meet?"

"My husband was an accountant. I assure you I'm financially sound."

Savannah smiled knowingly and nodded. "Listen, again, I'm sorry to come over here so late, but I really need to talk to you. My sleep schedule is all mixed up nowadays. Looks like yours is too."

Merry swallowed hard and sat on the opposite end of the couch. She had to force her gaze to remain on Savannah's wide eyes, rather than her stomach. Unable to wait any longer, she asked, "Is this about Joshua?"

Do I dare hope—part of my Joshua lives on?

"Yes. I've been holding on to it for months now, second-guessing myself each time I picked up the phone to call you. I wanted to give you enough time to grieve before I..."

Merry tried to keep her voice light, soft. She let her gaze fall to Savannah's stomach. "It's okay, honey. I think I might already know what it is."

Savannah's eyes widened, and then a sad smile crossed her lips. "Oh, no, do you think? This isn't...I mean...oh, goodness. This isn't Joshua's baby."

The emotional blow was so painful it felt like someone kicked her right in the solar plexus. Merry dug her nails into her palms, forcing herself not to show any outward emotion. Voice tight, she responded. "So then what brought you to my neck of the woods so late?"

Clearing her throat, Savannah took another drink of water. She reached into the purse at her feet and pulled out a spiral notebook. "Two weeks before Joshua passed, he showed up at my apartment. I was surprised because I hadn't seen him in over a year, and was shocked at his appearance. He looked so healthy, like he'd traveled back in time to high school. You know, right before his accident? He'd put on weight, got some color back..."

Merry interrupted, "Yes, I'm well aware. Go on."

Savannah's voice hitched as tears hung in the back of her throat. "I sort of freaked out, excited to see him clean and sober, but kind of afraid of him at the same time. I mean, I was, and still am, seeing someone else." Savannah patted her belly. "I thought maybe Joshua wanted to get back together."

Did Joshua try to resurrect their relationship and Savannah shot him down? Is that what sent him back to the needle?

Merry couldn't stop the words from flying out of her mouth. "And did he?"

Savannah shook her head. "No, he didn't. He came to apologize for all the mess he put me through. He asked me to forgive him for some of the nastier things that went down between the two of us before we broke up. Said making amends to those he'd harmed was all part of the nineth step to recovery."

"You came to my house six months after he died, in the middle of the night, to tell me that?"

Tears sprang into Savannah's eyes at the harsh tone. "No, I came to give you this," she whispered, sliding the binder over to Merry. "I can't even begin to imagine how hard all this is on you, and I'm so very sorry to dredge up painful memories. But I made a promise to Joshua that night to not only keep this notebook, but give it to you if something ever happened to him. He made me swear."

For a moment, Merry felt lightheaded. She stared at the blue cover, the words *To Hell and Back: One High at a Time* scrawled across the front in Joshua's handwriting.

"After I agreed, he calmed down a bit. He told me how he'd been clean for months and then took me outside and showed me his new motorcycle. Joshua tried to take me for a ride, but I told him I couldn't, since I was pregnant. He said he loved working at his dad's office. He seemed so, well, not exactly happy, but at peace. I finally got my nerve up to ask him what was in the notebook, and why he wanted me to watch it. He got this really strange look on his face. He said the less I knew the better."

Blood pounded in Merry's ears, making Savannah's words seem mumbled and distant. She couldn't stop staring at Joshua's scribble. In a low whisper, she asked, "What took you so long?"

Savannah seemed to sense the shift of the room's energy level. She stood and responded, "Honestly, I forgot about it. After Joshua left that night, I stashed it in the back of my closet under some old clothes. Didn't want my fiancé to find it. Plus, I figured Joshua would change his mind and come back for it later, you know, after whatever he was worried about was over. When he passed away, I was shocked. It didn't help my morning sickness decided to peak then, either. I had it with me at the funeral, but then…"

My Harold keeled over in front of everyone and left me alone to deal with this nightmare. Just like he did while Joshua was still alive. Yes, I remember. God, how I remember.

"Yeah, I get it."

Swiping at the tears running down her cheeks, Savannah continued. "I'm sorry I upset you, Mrs. Hall. I guess I hoped giving you his journal wouldn't be so painful now. I see I was wrong. Please know I never read it, and if I may be so bold, you shouldn't either. We both already know how Joshua was when he was using…"

Seething fury burned through Merry's mind. Unable to stop herself, she exploded. "You don't know the half of how he was, Savannah. You bailed out way too early, just like everyone else in his life. Don't you dare assume you knew anything about my son! I don't recall you ever staying up for days with him while he threw his fucking guts up from detoxing! Or wiping his brow while the shakes were so severe I thought his teeth would crack. Did you ever hold him while he begged you to let him die? Listen to him sob as he wished he'd never been born because he'd hurt too many people? It was my heart that died bit by bit with each trip to rehab, not yours. I watched my child, my own flesh and blood, suffer in ways I can't even explain—and no one was there to help me through it! Everyone gave up on him except me. So go, live your new life. Enjoy parenthood. It's a fucking blast—and not for the faint at heart. Hope your baby's daddy has a strong ticker. Mine didn't."

Openly sobbing, Savannah turned and wobbled as fast as her protruding belly allowed down the stairs. Merry waited until she heard the girl's vehicle leave before she moved an inch. If she had the capacity to feel sympathy any longer, she would have felt some for Savannah. The girl didn't deserve the brunt of her anger, but controlling her mouth these days proved to be more and more difficult.

Having a brief taste of hope appear only to be cruelly doused, made the crack in her psyche widen.

She ran her fingers over the worn cover, releasing the faint scent of her son. Dueling emotions battled for control. Part of her wanted to fix a pot of coffee and stay up all night reading, discovering the innermost thoughts, struggles, and feelings of her only child. The other part wanted to do exactly what Savannah had done—hide it away and forget it existed. If she opened it up and read it now, would she be able to handle it? Or would the words set in stone her decision to turn into a vicious killer?

Pulling the notebook to her chest, Merry held on tight. It took her a minute to realize she had been rocking back and forth.

Joshua. My baby...

No, she wouldn't read it now. She couldn't take any more emotional upheaval at the moment. What she needed was a release—something on which to vent her unending pain.

Merry stood and started pacing, hands clenching and unclenching. Pressure pulsed in her temples, making her vision blur and head throb. She heard her heartbeat thrum in her ears and felt the tightness in her chest.

Maniacal Merry roared to life and took control of her body, mind, and soul.

"Fuck waiting until Monday. Mookie, your time just expired."

10

One block before she reached 8th Street, Merry slowed down to a brisk walk. Light rain coated the dark streets as thunder rumbled in the distance. She stopped and scanned the area. No one was out and about. The threat of potential storms and high humidity seemed to convince most to stay inside.

Well, not everyone.

Crouching between two parked cars on the street, she removed the backpack. It was time she donned her next look.

She pulled on the black Lycra top. Shoved her hair inside the matching skullcap and then yanked off her running shoes, replacing them with boots. It took several tries to slide the gloves on over her swollen, bandaged knuckles.

If they don't fit, you must acquit!

Gloves secured after three attempts, she extracted the knife and repacked the bag.

A bolt of bright light skittered across the dark sky, followed seconds later with a loud boom of thunder. Merry slung the pack on her back and took off at a light trot, careful not to misstep on the slick pavement.

She kept to the shadows, away from the streetlights. Less than two minutes later, she was close enough to Mookie's house to have a clear view. Faint sounds of an argument between at least two people rose from behind her, though three houses away, she didn't worry. Still, just to be safe, Merry paused in mid-stride next to a large pile of trash while she watched her target's place.

Mookie was on the front porch, but he wasn't alone. Two young women flanked him on each side, and all three sat on the top step. Even from a distance, Merry could tell they were all higher than hot air balloons. Judging by the skimpy attire of the two girls, they were either pros or whores-in-training. They were entertaining themselves by taunting Hercules. With each rock Mookie tossed at the dog, the girls giggled. The one on Mookie's right even chunked a few.

Scanning the street once more, Merry waited until another bolt of lightning flashed. She stood and burst from her position when the thunder followed. Hopping the fence two doors down from Mookie's place, she jogged through the backyards of his neighbors. When she got to the fence surrounding Mookie's yard, she paused to listen and readjust her pack. Faint laughter and mutterings drifted in the air.

Mookie and his ho-down partners were still living it up.

At Hercules' expense.

Merry was over the fence and across the small space in seconds. She made it to the tiny back porch before the light misting transformed into a downpour. The old house rattled when three sets of feet pounded on the front porch.

Two sets went one way, and one the other.

Good! The entertainment left. Lucky them.

With her back pressed against the side of the house, Merry could hear Mookie muttering inside the kitchen. She turned and jumped off the porch. Squatting down, she reached into her pack, grabbing what she needed.

In the pouring rain, she moved toward the front yard. She spotted Hercules cowering under the front porch, the rope stretched to its limit. Merry tossed a full pound of fresh ground chuck at the dog. It landed inches from his nose. With the knife in her other hand, she bent down and sliced through the thick rope staked into the damp ground.

There you go, buddy. Eat some but don't get too full. Dessert is just around the corner.

Merry turned and ran toward the back porch. Once she reached the corner of the house, she smelled it. The heavy, thick vapor coated the night air.

Weed. Perfect!

She edged her way closer to the corner and then stole a quick peek. Sure enough, Mookie sat on the back porch smoking a blunt, the back door wide open.

Glancing behind her to make sure Hercules was still otherwise occupied, Merry let her breath out slow and easy. She didn't know how long Mookie would remain on the back porch. The underlying fear of the dog deciding to announce her presence by barking or even come out from his hiding spot and try to rip her throat out, made her heart rate spike.

"Yo, Mookie! I left my purse. Let me in, it's pouring out here!"

Merry froze at the sound of the shrill voice from the front. Grateful to be shielded from the front and back doors, two things hit her at once: Hercules didn't bark at the appearance of another person, and the sound of Mookie's footsteps tromping through the house.

She stole another peek.

The back door was still open.

The justice gods smile once again.

Grabbing her bag of tricks from its resting spot, Merry lunged from her position and up to the back porch. Making sure to keep her steps light and quiet, she inched onto the porch and quickly stepped over the rotted threshold. Her options were a short hallway leading to the living room/kitchen or a door on either side. She assumed one led to a bedroom and the other a bathroom.

Merry tried both. The door on her left was the bathroom, and the one on the right was to the bedroom. Yanking a dirty towel from the bathroom, she wiped up the water on the floor. Opening the bedroom door, Merry gave it a quick scan to make sure the small area was empty.

It was.

Setting the pack down on the floor, Merry pressed her ear against the wall and listened. The front door slammed, followed by heavy steps down the hall. Gripping the knife tighter, Merry tensed. Excitement coursed through her veins. She readied herself to pounce if the piece of shit opened the door.

He didn't.

"Fucking rain! Ruined a great night. No pussy and no more smack!"

Merry heard the chair on the back porch creak when Mookie plopped down. The door was only a few feet away, and Merry heard him attempt to light another go-around with the joint. In seconds, the scent of skunk edged its way through the door jam.

Less than a minute later, the back door slammed shut.

"Damn but I gotta piss!"

Merry sheathed the knife and reached out, wrapping her fingers around the doorknob. With slow, precise movements, she began to twist. When a sliver big enough to look through appeared, she could see enough to confirm Mookie was, indeed, using the bathroom.

Time to get my high on!

Merry burst from the bedroom. In three quick steps, she had Mookie around the neck before his own hand had a chance to release his johnson.

Muscle memory from years of karate kicked in. With her left arm around his neck, his trachea crushed against the bend of her elbow, Merry clamped her left hand on her bicep. She slammed her right palm on Mookie's shoulder while pushing her elbows together with everything she had. Her biceps and arm bone executed the perfect blood choke.

Even though he was wasted, Mookie tried in vain to fight back. Merry was surprised by the strength of such a scrawny bastard. His feet scrambled for traction while both arms flopped around like an oxygen-depleted fish. One flail landed a solid smack against Merry's eye socket.

She welcomed the pain. It made her flex ever harder, and in seconds, Mookie was unconscious. His limp body dropped to the floor with a loud *thud*.

Dashing back to the pack in the bedroom, she yanked out a short length of thin nylon rope. In seconds, Mookie's wrists were bound. He wouldn't be out much longer, so Merry slid her arms underneath his shoulders and dragged him to the living room. When she stopped, she let go and laughed when his head slammed into the floor. The impact made him moan while he returned to consciousness.

Before he was fully awake, Merry surveyed the living room. Sure enough, a nine millimeter rested on the kitchen table, right next to a cell phone. She snatched the weapon up, made sure it was loaded and the safety off and then tucked it in her waistband. The cell phone went into her back pocket. Side-stepping Mookie's body on the floor, she moved to the front door and locked it. She noticed all the white powder she'd dumped earlier was, indeed, gone.

"My head! What the fu..?"

Merry was by Mookie's side in a flash, the tip of the sharp knife pressed against his throat before he could finish his sentence. "Make a sound and it will be the last thing you do, Mr. Majors. Got it?"

Mookie's chocolate-colored eyes were wide pools of fear and confusion. A small gasp of recognition was the only noise in the living room. He clamped his mouth shut and nodded once.

Merry stood and stepped back, snatching the lone chair from its spot by the card table. She set it less than four feet from the front door. "You look uncomfortable, Mr. Majors. How about you get up and have a seat right there, huh? Should make our little question and answer session easier to concentrate on."

She watched Mookie's gaze dart to the kitchen table. The panic in his eyes grew as the realization his weapon and cell were no longer around hit home.

"Looking for this?" Merry brandished the gun.

Mookie's only response was a sharp intake of breath.

"I said have a seat, Mookie. Now." Merry pointed the gun at his chest. "Don't make me ask questions twice or you won't make it out of this alive."

She watched with twisted amusement. It took Mookie a few tries, but he finally rolled over onto his knees and stood. On wobbly legs, he stumbled across the floor and flopped onto the rickety chair.

Merry moved over and leaned against the kitchen doorway. She waited a few seconds to speak, enjoying the emotions streaking across Mookie's face. "So, let's start our visit off with establishing a few ground rules, shall we?"

Mookie didn't flinch.

"Now, what did I say about making me ask questions twice? Oh, I know what it is! You're confused about my previous statement to remain quiet. I'm giving you conflicting instructions, aren't I? Let me clarify. It's fine for you to answer my questions...expected, actually. Just no yelling for help or other such nonsense. Okay?"

Through clenched teeth, Mookie responded, "Got it."

Merry let a wide grin appear. "Fantastic! Okay, so rules one and two have been established. Rule number three is simple to remember. If you lie to me, I'll redecorate your door a lovely mixture of red and gray after I blow your brains out. Understand?"

"Yeah."

"What a cooperative little dirtbag you are, Mr. Majors! My dad always said even the most hardened criminals had an Achilles heel. The trick was learning to find it, and his favorite way was with a billy club. I prefer deadlier toys. Fair warning: I'm really not in a good mood, so I suggest you don't piss me off. Believe me when I say you won't like the end result."

"Look, if you're here for some product, I'm all out of..."

Merry laughed so hard, tears leaked from her eyes. "Oh, that's rich! Trying to save your ass by offering me drugs! Priceless!"

Mookie furrowed his brow in confusion. "I don't understand. You ain't here to score or rob me of my stash?"

"On the contrary. I'm here to score, just not what you think.

I want information. Give me what I want and I'll consider an alternate ending for you."

Sweat dripped down into Mookie's eyes. He blinked several times to clear his vision. "Information? Oh, I knew it! You're a cop! I done told y'all, I don't know shit about the next shipment! I..."

Mookie's mouth clamped shut when Merry chambered a round. She stepped forward and aimed right in between his bulging eyes. "You just broke rule number three, Mr. Majors."

"Wait, wait!" Mookie yelled, fidgeting in the chair.

"This is your only save, so make it count. Tell me about the shipment. The one you discussed in length via texts with Peppy."

Mookie's legs shook with nervous tremors. "Oh, Jesus...I can't. I just can't. You don't understand....He'll kill me. Make life for my moms awful."

"Enlighten me or die," Merry growled.

She watched the look of sheer terror on the bastard's face. His lips were trembling, and he began to hyperventilate. Saw the dark stain of urine soak through his shorts. Merry decided to keep him off balance and switch interview tactics before the little wimp passed out from fright.

"Breathe, Mr. Majors. You're depleting the oxygen levels in your brain, which will make it harder to recall things. Might make you lie to me again, which would be very unfortunate for you. So, while you get yourself under control, let me give you a bit of background information. It'll help you understand exactly what I want, and why I will get it. Fair enough?"

Closing his eyes, throat muscles undulating when he swallowed, Mookie nodded.

Merry stepped back to her original position against the wall. "I told you on my visit here earlier, I'm not a cop. And since I'm asking you to be honest here, I'll do the same. I'm not a dealer, either. I'm simply a mother seeking revenge for her son's murder, one rung up the ladder at a time."

Mookie's eyelids shot open. "Murder? Lady, you got the wrong guy! I ain't never killed no one! I swear!"

Merry raised an inquisitive eyebrow. "That tattoo on your

back says otherwise. Southern Folks full membership insignia, right?"

"It ain't real! I mean, it's a real tat, but it's a fake. Had it done at some backdoor parlor in Pensacola a few years back. Thought it would keep me safe, you know, from other bangers. Moms made me promise to stay outta the gangs, so I've been faking for years! I swear lady, if you're looking for the dude who killed your kid, you've got the wrong guy!"

"Oh, I don't think so. You and other fucking scumbags like Peppy, kill people everyday. It's a slow, agonizing death from the poison you sell. The cops can't stop it. The courts are worthless, letting liberal bullshit agendas dictate their rulings. Someone needed to step up and take the trash out, which is what I'm doing. Peppy's product took my only child's life. Turned my boy into a raging junkie, and when my son's heart quit beating, my husband's stopped soon after. What you do for a living destroyed my world. Rather than get a legitimate job and contribute to society, you deplete it. I'm not the only person who's lost someone, but I'm different because I chose to make a permanent difference. So, I decided to make Peppy and all his cohorts pay the ultimate price. An eye for an eye, a life for a life is my motto now. It was quite liberating when I bashed his skull in. If you don't want to suffer the same fate, don't lie to me again."

Blinking twice to absorb the words, Mookie choked out, "You killed...oh, shit, you really ain't a cop, are you?"

A crooked smile creased Merry's lips while she shook her head. She could see the twerp connecting all the dots. Trying to get his neurons to fire on all cylinders and process what she'd just said. His eyes widened even further, mouth agape. Merry assumed he'd just realized he was in danger of losing his life at any moment and came to terms with the fact the woman in front of him was beyond crazy.

Mookie choked out, "Fuck! I have seen you before! In court the other day! You're the mom of that kid who died in the alleyway...oh, Jesus. Oh, Jesus! I warned Peppy about all this."

This time, Merry pulled the knife from its sheath. She held it up to the light, admiring the shards of silver light reflecting off the smooth, sharp surface. Before Mookie had a chance to take in a gulp of air to finish his thoughts, she was right in front of him. The stench of his fear, urine, and lack of personal hygiene made her nose twitch. Jerking her arm forward, she stopped just shy of piercing through the thin shorts that housed his flaccid dick.

"His name was Joshua Robert Hall, not 'that kid,' and yes I work for the judge. Made finding out information on you much easier. Now, tell me all about this shipment coming in from Memphis and every single thing you know about your supplier. You mentioned Tee earlier. You've got twenty seconds before I castrate you. Go."

"Oh shit, okay, okay! T-Dog, that's my guy. Don't know his real name, I swear. We ain't friends or nothing. Met him in lockup about five years ago when he got busted for a DUI. Knew right away he was a junkie, and we partnered up not long after. Told me he had access to a lot of cash and connections that would keep us out of prison."

"Description, please?" Merry queried while watching sweat drip off Mookie's chin.

Mookie swallowed hard, and Merry could see the hairs standing up on his arms. It took him a few seconds to find his voice. "Tall, skinny white kid. Blond hair, green eyes. Has money and drives a silver Tahoe."

"How does the delivery go down?"

"When the stuff arrives, we go get it and come back here to cut it up. Makes us all more money that way. I never know exactly when it arrives, just that it's coming. I wait until T-Dog sends me a snap video and then head out to wherever he tells me to meet him. We use coded messages–keeps things safe. Please, lady, I get your reasons. I do. But I'm begging you, please stop. You're stepping into some shit you don't wanna be in."

Just when Merry was about to ask a question, Mookie's phone chimed. She backed up and yanked it from her pocket.

"That's T-Dog's ringtone. Watch it...I swear I'm not lying. Not kidding about the shit storm you're about to..."

Gesturing with the knife, Merry grumbled. "Shut up. Oh, looks like I'm about to put a face to the name, huh? Snap video?

The kind that disappears once viewed, right? How very high-tech of you two!" Merry scrolled through the phone. She clicked on the new video icon and brought it up. It took a few seconds to load, but once it did, the world seemed to stop.

The voice was full of excitement as the recording started. "Dude! Haven't seen you in ages! Need to kick it tomorrow night! I'll buy the beer. You bring the movies! Same bat time, same bat channel! Peace!"

Merry's brain didn't want to believe what it just witnessed. The shock of seeing Tad's familiar face took control of her body for only a few seconds. Unable to look anymore, or completely comprehend how this latest twist would affect things, she shoved the phone back into her pocket.

What happened next was all a blur.

The sudden impact of Mookie's bound arms against the side of her face made stars dance in her line of vision. She felt her body fly backward, her ass landing with a hard thump on the ground while the knife skittered across the floor. Somehow, she managed to keep her balance and not fall all the way flat on her back. There was no time to concentrate on the burning, red-hot pain when she felt the heaviness of Mookie's body plunge into hers.

"I'm gonna kill you, bitch!" Mookie swore, landing on top of her.

Merry never responded. They rolled across the hardwood. On autopilot, her muscles kicked in. When their bodies stopped moving, she was on top of him. Using her elbow, she brought it down on the bridge of his nose. Mookie grunted in pain when blood exploded in all directions. She followed the direct hit by jumping to her feet. Before the bastard had a chance to stand up, Merry kicked him with all her strength in the kidney.

The pain rendered him mute, a frozen scream stuck on his bloodied lips. Merry grabbed the knife. In one swift motion she sliced through the rope. Mookie groaned again but didn't move.

Merry leaned down and slit the bastard's throat. "Forgot to mention rule number four: try to hurt me and you're dog food."

In a dazed rush, Merry picked up the rope. She set the gun back on the kitchen table, grabbed the pack, and then shoved the bloody blade and rope inside. She watched Mookie sputter and struggle for air, his hands soaked in blood while he tried in vain to stop the bleeding. Moving past him, she could hear the sounds of scratching and growling at the front door.

After glancing back at the nearly dead Mookie, Merry turned her head and whispered into the door-jam. "Hercules? Here boy. Daddy wants to play!"

She unlocked the front door, opening it wide, making sure to stay behind it. The rain-soaked dog didn't need any urging or encouragement to come inside. Hercules smelled the weakness. Knew his prey was down for the count. The pit bull lunged from the doorway, landing right on top of Mookie. Merry watched in utter fascination while the dog's head shot forward and latched on to the neck and shook, tearing chunks of flesh off.

Arching her body and using the backpack for a shield, Merry moved to the other side of the door, closing it fast. Once on the porch, she paused to listen to the sounds of Hercules shredding his former master to pieces.

Ah, sweet payback. Enjoy your dessert, Hercules.

The cooling droplets of rain were a relief helping to calm her bruised cheeks. Merry broke out into a run, her mind spinning. The discovery of the identity of the next rung in the ladder made her mouth dry and knees weak.

She was angry at herself for not following protocol, for allowing herself to succumb to the emotional duress and veer from the plan. It was a stupid, stupid mistake. Her mindset had been controlled by emotions rather than stealth. Cockiness, and the need to satiate the sorrow took over, and it almost got her killed.

Merry ignored her sore muscles and pushed her legs to their limits. The knowledge her next kill wouldn't be some random stranger wasn't something she'd even remotely considered. She needed to be at home—safe—so she could digest this new development.

Merry shook her head at the strange twist of events.

Sorry Judge Tompkins, but you're about to become a member of my club now. Tad is next on my list.

11

4:15 A.M. SUNDAY MORNING

Sprinting down the street, Merry finally stopped in front of the last house before the intersection of 8th and Markham. No lights were on in the house, and the streetlamp was on the fritz. Plus, a big land-yacht-looking car had parked next to the curb while she'd been playing with Mookie. Less than three feet behind it was an old truck. Numerous garbage bags were stacked on top of each other, spilling out over the curb and into the street. She smiled. It was a perfect place to hide and change clothes.

Dawn wasn't far away, and she couldn't be seen running down the street in her current outfit. The boots went first, followed by the soaking wet top and skullcap. She shoved it all back into the bag. She nearly screamed when a cell phone chimed in her pocket.

What in the world? Oh, damn! I can't have this on me!

She jerked Mookie's phone from her pocket, shocked she didn't recall putting it there. Grateful it only beeped once—an indicator it was a text—she tried to find the mute button. Her gloves were wet, and though she tried to hang on, the phone slipped out from her fingers. The sound of the screen shattering when it landed on the pavement made her cringe.

Snatching it back up, Merry scanned the destroyed, useless front. Tamping down her irritation, she convinced herself she didn't need it. Though she didn't know the location where Mookie was to meet up with Tad Tompkins, she knew where Tad lived. Her next recon missions would center on following him for several days, learning his daily habits.

One annoying detail solved, she stared at the phone. There was no way she'd take it back, even if all she did was get close enough so she could toss it into Mookie's front yard. She couldn't copy the information over to the burner phone in her bag either, since the front touch screen was destroyed. It was too dark to remove the back and see if it housed a memory card, and she couldn't risk using the flashlight in her bag.

The only choice left was to remove the battery and then bury both it and the dead phone deep inside one of the plastic garbage bags. It took longer in the dark to pop the back cover off, and the intense pressure in her forehead didn't help. The stab of pain wasn't from getting clocked by Mookie. It was a warning sign: a migraine was less than an hour away. Not only did she need to get the hell out of the area but also take her medication before she was blinded by the overwhelming pain.

"Come on; come on!" Merry whispered in frustration. She let out a huff of air when the back finally came off. Scooting over to the pile of trash, she forced herself not to gag from the stench while she felt around. In seconds, she found one near the bottom with a loose drawstring. She shoved the phone and the battery down deep inside.

Then she heard it.

A weird sound she didn't recognize.

Heart pounding, Merry removed the gloves and shoved them inside the backpack. Bracing her palms on the wet ground, she spun around and found herself inches from the bloody snout of a large dog.

Oh, the irony! My death certainly isn't coming the way I

envisioned! Not even close. Can't believe I didn't shut the door all the way! What an enormous cluster-fuck this has been! Damn you, Savannah!

Instead of shaking in fear and releasing some funky pheromone only a canine could smell, Merry laughed.

Hard.

A bitter, fuck-my-life cackle while she waited to be ripped to shreds.

The streetlight made an odd humming noise, flickered twice, and then stayed on. Merry could see the big dog's eyes staring at her. Hercules breathed hard, a thick strand of saliva intermixed with blood hung from his jaws. He didn't growl, didn't bare his teeth, and his hackles weren't raised. The rope she'd sliced through earlier trailed behind him. Merry figured that was the strange noise she'd heard.

"Guess you've never read the one about the lion and the mouse, huh? I would be the mouse in this situation. Wouldn't eat my brains if I were you. They're too damaged to be any good."

A long, pink tongued tinged in red appeared. Hercules licked his lips and then sat with an unceremonious *plop* on the pavement. His tail thumped the ground. A smile appeared on Merry's lips when she realized he actually wagged it. She sensed no aggression from the dog at all.

"Well, this certainly wasn't part of my plan. Yet another reason not to leave the house when angry, huh? Seems you aren't going to eat me...at least not yet...so what now? Can't really leave you out here because—and don't take this personally—I don't know what you'll do when Animal Control comes around. Or worse. Some kid running to catch the school bus..."

Merry's comments were cut short when a beam of light appeared from the opposite end of the street. A deep, throaty rumble of an engine made her pulse quicken. She had a major decision to make in only seconds. Leave and hope the dog didn't attack anyone, including her, or grab the end of the rope and take off for her car, man-eating dog in tow.

She peeked around the trunk, scanning both directions.

Her heart rate tripled when she saw a truck. It had stopped two houses down from Mookie's and turned the headlights off. Merry took a deep breath and whispered, "Okay boy. You either come with me or end up at the pound. I promise I will never hurt you, so please reciprocate. Oh, and no barking."

Hercules responded by increasing the speed of his wagging tail.

Merry reached back and grabbed the pack. With one final glance down at the dog, she took off, Hercules trotting in silence right next to her.

I'll be damned.

❋ ❋ ❋

Ten minutes later, just as the yellow rays of the morning sun appeared in the horizon, Merry was at her car. After opening the trunk and tossing the pack inside, she rummaged around until she found two large beach towels.

Hercules was about two feet behind her, panting, watching her every move. She unlocked the passenger door, arranged the towels in the seat, and then patted her thighs. "Come on, boy. Don't be scared."

With tentative steps, Hercules moved forward until he was close enough to sniff out the interior. Merry sensed his unease as he let out a low whine. Surprised he'd come this far, yet fearful of being caught with him, Merry's next move was risky. She leaned over him and patted the front seat.

"I'm sure trust is a major issue for you, but come on now! I released you, gave you food, and let you get some revenge. What more do you want? We've got to go! Hop up there...please?"

Maybe it was her tone. Maybe it was the fact that on some weird, unexplainable level, they'd connected. After all, Merry had embraced her own dark side, releasing her inner animal, so perhaps Hercules picked up on the vibe. It could have been the desperation, the sense of hopelessness, the inborn drive to survive and kill their enemies. Whatever it was binding the man-eater with the man-killer, it didn't matter to Merry. What mattered was Hercules taking in one final sniff and then jumping into the front seat.

"There you go! That's a good boy!"

After tossing the rope-leash onto the floorboard, Merry shut the door. She ran to the other side and climbed behind the wheel. The poor dog reeked. Judging by its filthy coat, Hercules had never had a bath. Add in the rusty scent of blood and the concoction was horrendous. Merry cranked up the engine, cracked the windows, and turned the air on full blast.

The collar around his neck was way too tight and had obviously never been taken off. To get it off would require the knife, which she would do at home.

"So, we good? You aren't going to attack while I'm driving, right?"

Hercules' tailed thumped against the door.

"Good! Okay, I'm taking you to your new home. Warning, when we get there, you're getting a bath. You stink."

Ignoring her, Hercules turned his head and stuck his nose through the opening, sniffing the early dawn air. Merry took it as the signal she just gained a new companion. Backing up, she pulled onto the road and headed home, just as the sun announced to the rest of the sleeping city it was morning.

12

Pulling into his neighborhood, Derek killed the headlights. It was a habit he'd watched his father do. Dad liked to say he performed a kindness to the neighbors by not disturbing them at odd hours when he returned home from the night shift.

Once in the driveway, Derek shut the engine off and gathered up items from the passenger seat. He was glad to be home. The last twenty-four-plus hours had been brutal. He needed to take a shower and wash the funk off, check on Stonewall, and then sleep for a good ten hours.

Stepping out into the already hot morning air, he groaned after looking at his truck. The hood and grill were covered in dead insects. He made a mental note to hand-wash it later before the corpses were permanently embedded in the paint.

Derek unlocked the front door and went inside, grateful for the change in air temperature. "Hey buddy! Miss me?"

Stonewall jumped around like a puppy, yipping and nipping at Derek's legs all the way into the kitchen. Derek checked the feeder, which was almost empty, and refilled it. The welcome home celebration ended as Stonewall buried his snout into the kibble.

Derek dropped his bag on the bed and began shedding clothes on his way to the bathroom. When he moved back in, he couldn't stand the idea of returning to his childhood room, so he took over the master bedroom. The creepy factor of that only seemed to bother him during times when he was exhausted—like right now—or on the rare occasion when he was ill.

The hot water and soap revived his tired body. As he scrubbed himself squeaky clean, he heard Stonewall push the door open. Through the frosted glass of the shower door, he saw the blur of black as his buddy did circles on the bathmat until he found a comfortable spot.

"I see how you are—eat first then visit. Don't expect any treats from me if I'm not number one in your life. Priorities, Stonewall. Priorities!"

Once finished and dried, Derek wrapped the towel around his waist. Bending down, he scooped up Stonewall and shut the bathroom light off. Though his clothes and furniture filled up the room, Derek never slept in the bed. Ever since he'd been little, Derek preferred to sleep on a couch, remote in hand, TV noise in the background. Stonewall knew the drill and wriggled in his arms.

Plopping down on the cool leather sofa, Derek flicked on the TV. The local news was on, the hot-as-hell new blonde weekend reporter—Charlotte? Cheryl?—was as perky as ever. Her bright blue eyes and pouty smile made Derek's heart skip a beat the first time she delivered news behind the shiny black desk. Most of the time, he didn't pay attention to what she said. Instead, he preferred to fantasize about what those lips would feel like on him.

"Damn." She reported live, the camera showing a wide-shot of her location, rather than a headshot of her. Then Derek's eyes widened. He thumbed up the volume.

Is she at...?

Stonewall jumped and started barking when Derek's cell

phone rang. He didn't have to look to see who was calling. The rock in his gut, set there by the images on the screen, already told him.

Mitch was calling about De'Shawn Majors.

Ignoring the phone, Derek focused his attention on the TV.

"...mauled body was found this morning by neighbors. Though the police have yet to provide any comments or statements, one neighbor told us the victim owned a dog, which has yet to be found. The name of the victim has yet to be released, pending notification of his next of kin..."

Muscles sore and mind spinning, Derek stood and walked to the bedroom. Pulling the phone from the bag, he called Mitch back. When his partner answered, Derek could tell he was on-scene. The noise level was ridiculous.

"Gee, did I catch you sleeping?" Mitch snarled.

"Haven't had any coffee this morning yet. Have you?" Derek pulled on a pair of briefs.

"Nope. Unlike you, I've been working. It's time you join me. This investigation is a nightmare. A real nightmare. I'm at..."

"I know—just caught it on the news. Is my favorite piece of eye-candy still tottering around scene in some spiky heels?"

"Don't know. Don't care. Just hurry up and get here. This one...well, this one is a fucking mess."

"Does that mean you don't want me to bring you some coffee and donuts?"

"Screw you, Derek," Mitch disconnected the call before Derek could say anything else.

Eyes burning and brain exhausted, Derek finished getting dressed. He wondered why in the hell he ever decided to follow in his father's footsteps.

It rounded out the top three biggest mistakes he'd ever made.

***

Derek parked a block away and shut the engine off. He gave a quick scan of the area, grateful no one was outside. A grim smile appeared when he considered the inhabitants of the entire three-block radius might all be gathered in front of 139 8th Street. After sliding on a ball cap and sunglasses, he exited the car and followed the sounds coming from one block over.

When he rounded the corner, just like he'd expected, a large crowd of about thirty people stood in the middle of the street in front of De'Shawn's house. Even from the distance, Derek felt the collective anger and shock. The emotional energy was palpable. The sun was out, and sweat beaded his brow. The stench of garbage hung in the damp air when he passed a large pile by the sidewalk.

He decided to cross the street and flank the crowd. Stepping off the curb, not paying any attention to his feet, his landed on a rock and stumbled, dropping his keys. Bending down to retrieve them, he saw bloody paw prints.

Glad I haven't eaten yet. Death by dog...this should interesting. That's what the bastard gets for having a canine big enough to inflict damage. Stonewall could maybe take out an ankle.

The grumbling and yelling reached a fevered pitch when Derek came up behind the crowd. A harried, fresh-faced recruit who looked like she should still be in high school held up her hand to stop him. Before she had a chance to speak, Derek flashed his neck badge. She gave him a weary smile and then turned her focus back to the group.

Derek ducked under the yellow police tape, looking around for Mitch. He knew his partner would be somewhere other than the actual crime scene, keeping his presence under the radar. The fear of being recognized was always on the minds of undercover cops. He noticed Mitch was on the front porch of De'Shawn's neighbor, dressed inconspicuously like Derek, his back to the throng of onlookers. Derek picked up his pace and joined them.

Mitch nodded his head toward Derek and said, "Excuse me, Mrs. Williams. I need to confer with my partner a moment. Please, take the time to get yourself a cold drink. Try to relax. It will help you recall things better."

"Sure thing, sir. Such a shame. I done told that boy to stop being so mean to poor Hercules. I *told* him! Oh, his mama is going to just die!" Mrs. Williams lamented before she went inside.

Derek followed Mitch to the opposite end of the porch.

"Took you long enough! Where've you been?" Mitch grumbled.

"You're in a shit mood. What, your hot girl turn cold or something?"

Mitch glared at Derek and then wiped a trickle of sweat from his chin. He blew out a huff of air and lowered his voice. "No. I'm cranky because the old broad can't remember squat...and because I hate dealing with Hudson. He's a prick. Already been up in my face about Mookie. Actually had the guts to ask me if I was stalking and killing informants on the side. Can you believe that shit?"

Derek tried not to laugh at the expression on Mitch's face. He recognized the seething anger behind the eyes and heard it in his voice. "Hudson has had a hard-on for you ever since you did the nasty with his main squeeze, so yeah, I can believe it. I think he'd spend every penny of his retirement pay on throwing a huge party if you weren't on the force anymore."

A snide grin curled up the corner of Mitch's mouth. "Girl was worth it. She needed to know what a real man was like in the sack."

Ignoring Mitch's favorite subject, Derek shifted gears. "So, what's going on? News hinted Mookie was mauled to death? I'm guessing they are actually reporting a snippet of truth since I stumbled upon some paw prints down the street. They sure looked like..."

"They were made from blood? Well that's because they were." Mitch leaned against the railing. "De'Shawn's throat is gone, along with part of his face and most of his fingers. I mean, I could see his spine...and he was face up on the floor. The living room is covered in red. Covered. House is clean of product so far, so could be he was robbed and then someone used the dog as a distraction. Or, it could be he had himself a party after getting sprung. Snorted it all up and then accidently got too close and became a chew toy. No signs of forced entry. Only thing of note missing is his cell. Oh, and the dog."

Derek glanced over Mitch's shoulder. He could see the dog wasn't anywhere around. "What, did the mutt chew through the rope...or pull the stake out of the ground?"

Mitch shook his head. "Nope. Someone cut it. Which pretty much rules out an accident."

The screen door squeaked when Mrs. Williams walked back outside, a tall glass of lemonade in her hands. Derek noticed they were still shaking. The poor old lady's gaze shifted between the two of them.

"Either of you like something to drink? Sorry I didn't ask before. My manners are shot. This is just, oh, I can't believe it!"

Out of the duo, Derek had a softer touch when interviewing. He knew that was why Mitch called him down since Derek wasn't Mookie's handler. Moving in front of Mitch, Derek smiled warmly at the elderly woman. "How kind of you, but no thank you. Mrs. Williams, wasn't it?"

"Yes, that's right."

"Let's have a seat over here and talk. Do you mind if I take notes?"

"Not at all, though I really don't have anything to add to what I already told him and the other man earlier." Mrs. Williams smiled, motioning toward Mitch with her head full of white hair. "I woke up early like I always do, took my trash out to the curb before it got too hot, and—oh, it was just—in all my days, I ain't never seen such a thing!"

Derek saw tears well up in her cloudy eyes. He urged Mrs. Williams to take a drink. "Forgive me if my questions are similar to what my partner already asked. I'm just trying to catch up here. Okay?"

"Yes, sir."

"Thank you." Derek smiled. "So here's the first set of questions. Did you see anyone outside before you discovered Mr. Majors? Hear any odd noises or notice any strange vehicles?"

Mrs. Williams shook her head no, her gaze no longer on Derek as she looked past him over to De'Shawn's. "And last night, the thunder was so loud, and I'm afraid of storms, so I took a sleeping pill."

"What time was that?"

"Um, I guess around nine or so. News wasn't on yet."

"I see. What about the last week or so? Do you recall anything odd...out of place around here? Notice any strangers?"

Mrs. Williams turned her attention back to Derek. She started to shake her head no but then took in a gasp of air. "Why yes...yes I do! The day De'Shawn came home from jail...I saw something. I surely did!"

Derek let a small grin appear, knowing the revelation irked the shit out of his partner. "Tell me, Mrs. Williams, what did you see?"

"Well, it was early evening, close to sunset. I was outside tending my roses when I saw De'Shawn hit poor Hercules over the head with a big piece of wood. He's always hurting that dog one way or another. Never could understand why he even had one! Poor thing was skinny as a rail. Used to bark all the time—which annoyed the entire block to no end—until De'Shawn had its vocal chords cut."

"He did what?" Mitch interrupted.

Derek shot Mitch a look strong enough to silence him. He motioned for Mrs. Williams to continue.

"Yep. At first, I just thought the dog was too scared of him to bark any more. One night, oh about eight months ago, the boy was high on something. Loosened his tongue. He was outside on the porch, talking real loud to nobody but Hercules. Said that he wasn't gonna have the cops called and get in trouble from the constant barking, so he fixed the problem."

"Jesus, what an ass," Mitch whispered.

"So, you witnessed Mr. Majors strike the dog? Then what happened?" Derek urged.

"Yes, that's right. I can't stand to see any animal abused, so I said something to him. I...oh, I uh..." Mrs. Williams clamped her mouth shut.

"It's okay, ma'am. Tell me. Did you two get into an argument? Exchange ugly words or something?"

Tears started to flow down her dark, wrinkled cheeks. Derek saw a look of remorse and fear behind her eyes. "I...told him if he didn't quit hitting Hercules, I'd come over and...and...and cut him loose in the middle of the night. But I swear I didn't mean it! It was just a threat...you know...to get him to stop? The guy who drove up on the bike must have heard me! Oh dear Jesus, God in Heaven! I gave him the idea!"

Derek's heart rate went into overdrive. "Mrs. Williams, what guy? Do you remember what he looked like?"

"Not really. Only caught a quick glance before I went back inside. White. Average height and sort of skinny. Kind of built like you." Mrs. Williams pointed at Mitch. "He did have some sort of ink on his right arm, but he was too far away for me to make out what it was."

Taken aback, Derek forced his voice to remain neutral. He could just imagine the look on Mitch's face. "What about hair color or any distinguishing features?"

Mrs. Williams shook her head. "Don't know. He still had a helmet on. I just remember thinking he was the healthiest looking junkie I'd seen in years."

Derek couldn't help but laugh. "Well that certainly answered another one of my questions, which was about whether you knew what Mr. Majors did for a living."

"Everyone around here knows what that boy does...er, did...to pay his bills. I've lived here for over thirty years, and I've seen more than my share of addicts walking up that porch. I sure have. Between his mama's shenanigans and eventually De'Shawn's, I know how to spot someone looking to score."

Derek shook his head, shocked by the woman's honesty. "So, when you said healthy, what did you mean?"

"My first impression was first-time user. Guy was thin and lean, like a basketball player, rather than stocky like a linebacker. Had sort of an...oh, what's the right word?...fancy-pants walk?"

"Do you mean he looked effeminate?"

"Oh, no. Just wasn't a burly tough guy. Looked like he worked out, but not to be huge...just healthy. Does that make sense?"

Derek scribbled the information down. He heard Mitch ask, "You said bike. Did you mean a motorcycle?"

"Yes. I remember hearing it rumble right before De'Shawn struck poor Hercules. It was loud. That's all I remember. Sorry."

Derek and Mitch didn't have a chance to ask any other questions. The crowd roared to life when Mookie's body was removed in a bag, shouting out for justice for De'Shawn.

13

7:15 A.M. SUNDAY MORNING

Yet another reason I bought a house in the freaking sticks! Privacy!

Merry stopped at the end of the long, curvy dirt road serving as the driveway. The new place she would be moving into in less than a week stared back in silence. She'd already made numerous trips with carloads full of small items during the last week, yet each time she arrived, a lump of tears appeared.

The quaint place would never be home.

It was a cute, one-story ranch with a wrap-around front porch, nearly a mile from the main road and nestled behind enormous pecan and oak trees. She'd purchased it, and the five acres it sat on, for a low price. The house had been on the market for almost two years after the previous owner passed away. When she originally toured the place, she understood why. The exterior had been updated with new vinyl siding, but the interior looked like something off the set of a 60s sitcom.

The property was bought for numerous reasons, including

its seclusion. Merry didn't need nosey neighbors observing her comings and goings. Now, the private area would serve another purpose—hiding her new companion, Cujo. Glancing over at Hercules, she chuckled. The window was full of slobber, the towels covered in dried blood.

"Come on, boy. I've got things to do before my head pops off."

Exiting the car, Merry stopped at the trunk first. She pulled out the knife from the pack and tucked it in her waist, just to be safe. After shutting the trunk, she walked over and opened the passenger door.

Hercules jumped out, his nose immediately on the ground, sniffing.

"Hang on, boy. Let's get this rope off, shall we?"

To her surprise, the dog stopped and stared at her. She held her hand out, backside first, and let him sniff it as she moved it toward him with slow, calculated movements.

"I'm sure I stink too, so don't judge me." She laughed. Hercules responded by licking her hand. "Good boy. Okay, hold still and let me get this thing off your neck."

While running her left hand over the top of the dog's chunky head, Merry slid the knife out. Cooing gibberish to him, she inched it toward the collar. In one quick slice, he was free. The filthy piece of material dropped to the ground.

Hercules wagged his tail and whined.

"There! You are really free now. So, our first order of business is a bath. Got to get all that evidence washed away. Let's do this the old fashioned way, shall we? Not sure how you'll do in the house, so come on. Follow me."

Merry walked to the rickety fence surrounding the house and unlocked the gate. Hercules followed, his nose back on the ground. When they reached the backyard, the big dog froze when the few ducks that had been swimming in the small pond took off, quacking away in fear.

Merry set the knife on the back porch railing and unlocked the door. "They're just birds, silly. No need to be afraid. Trust me—they are more terrified of you. Hang on while I get some soap."

The first thing she grabbed was her migraine pills from her purse, followed by a glass of water. Downing them, she returned to the porch, bottle of dish soap in tow. She made her way to the edge of the water, hoping Hercules would follow. He was several steps behind her, his eyes taking in everything. Merry could tell he was shaking.

Sitting down at the edge, Merry quickly disposed of her running shoes and clothes. When she turned around, Hercules was still sitting in the same spot.

Merry stood and walked into the water up to her knees, making plenty of noise to scare away any snakes lurking about. "I told you in the car you needed a bath. Wasn't kidding when I said you stink. I promise it's okay. I used to be afraid of the water too, but look at me now!"

Holding her breath, Merry went under. The water wasn't exactly cold, yet it was still refreshing, and the sudden change in temperature helped ease the throbbing in her forehead. When she popped back up, she burst out laughing.

Hercules was right at the edge, his feet millimeters from the water. He whined and paced back and forth—she assumed searching for her. Merry moved closer to the bank. "Oh, it's okay big guy. It feels good, I promise. Haven't lied to you yet, have I? If you let me get you cleaned up, I'll let you come inside while I find you something to eat, okay? I need someone to watch over me while I sleep, which is going to happen soon."

Though probably from her friendly tone—and not from some strange, mystical connection—Hercules seemed to understand her words. He took two steps forward and then bent his head down and lapped at the water. After a few good licks, his back haunches tightened, and he jumped in. The natural instinct to paddle kicked in. He snorted water from his nose, and he swam around in a circle. In seconds, he was chest deep in the water next to Merry.

Unsure how long he would hold still, she squirted the dish soap onto his back and started scrubbing. Between the warm sun, cool water, and caring touches, woman and beast bonded.

"Bath's over. Let's go get you something to eat and then situated for a while. You did pretty well in the car, so let's try the house next. I've got to rest before my head explodes."

Hercules shook his coat once again before he followed. Merry had spent the last fifteen minutes sprawled out on the grass, air-drying, while Hercules checked out his new home. The pain in her head had abated for a few minutes but then roared back. Merry feared she wouldn't make to the house before puking. Gathering up her clothes, she stood and headed to the house, a four-legged buddy at her side.

"Bet you didn't know you're named after a mythical legend who killed his wife and children and then was forced to perform twelve labors to redeem himself, did you? Hmm, that was your old life, and you need another name for your new life. Oh, what's the name of the guy who killed Medusa? Ah yes! Perseus. How about that?"

Once inside, she propped the back door open, just in case. Merry laughed when the dog let out a weird whine. "Okay, you're right. Too formal. How about simply Percy? Yes! That sounds right. Percy."

Percy stayed right at the edge of the door, hesitant to step fully inside. Merry pulled a bowl from the cabinet along with a can of tuna and fixed Percy a late breakfast. When she bent down to set the bowl on the floor, red-hot pain lanced through her head, making her dizzy. Another stabbing blow took her breath away. Bursts of yellow and orange distorted her vision. She vomited and collapsed on the floor.

In the distance, she heard the bowl crash against the tiles along with a low yelp from Percy. Merry tried to stand up—to move—but all she could do was curl into a ball, her palms crushed against her ears. Tears of anger and terror raced down her cheeks.

Come on, pills, come on! Kick in! Oh, God, I can't...stand...this.

Drifting...She was drifting away. The sounds and smells of the kitchen vanished. Her mind disengaged from the overwhelming pain. Dancing on the sharp edge between consciousness and sleep, disturbing visions swam inside Merry's mind.

She was helpless to stop them.

❖❖❖

Joshua stood in the doorway, his once strong physique transformed into a walking cadaver. Flat, dead eyes stared at them like they were strangers. His clothes hung limp on his thin frame, like he was still a child wearing his father's shirt and pants. Body language full of defiance and anger, Joshua turned and walked away, duffel bag slung over his shoulder. "I'm outta here."

"Son, please! You need help. Let me make a few phone calls...get you a bed at..." Merry begged.

"You'll do no such thing. He's already been three times, Merry! Insurance won't pay for any more treatments. If he wants to get a taste for what life is really like—on his own without you coddling him every minute—then let him go. He's a grown man, and we can't stop him. Can't force him to get clean. That he has to do—to want—on his own. Honestly, I'm sick of dealing with this shit."

"Harold!"

Voice louder, Harold continued. "Joshua, if you want to destroy your life, that's completely in your hands. Not ours. Until you get yourself together, don't come back to this house. Next time you show up here high, I'll call Derek and have you arrested."

Ignoring Harold's rant, Merry pushed past her annoyed spouse. She reached out for Joshua's arm just as he opened the front door. "Son...don't do this. Don't walk away. You're dad's just angry..."

"Damn right I'm angry! The boy is over twenty-one and has done nothing with his life except get high! Oh, and wreck his car, lose his license, bring trash into my house! You do realize drug dealers know where we live now, Merry, don't you?"

"Screw you! The minute I broke my leg, I've been nothing

more than a financial burden to you, Dad," Joshua spat out, a hint of red dotting his pale cheeks. "Once I wasn't the star football player anymore, I ceased to exist."

Harold lunged for Joshua. Merry saw the fury, rage, shame, and heartache glinting in his eyes. She stepped in between father and son. Both men were screaming at each other, with Merry caught in the middle. Harold and Joshua were livid, and before she could calm either of them down, or duck in time, the punch landed.

Harold's fist slammed into her mouth, and the impact left her dazed—but only for a second. "Enough! Both of you!" Merry screamed, holding her hand under her face to catch the dripping blood. "All this isn't helping one bit! We need to sit down—talk about this as a family—just like they suggested in counseling..."

"No, Mom. We don't. There's nothing left to discuss."

In a flash, Joshua turned and disappeared into the darkness. Merry and Harold stood on the front porch and watched him climb into the passenger seat of a waiting car, silent tears racing down both their cheeks. Stunned, and fearful it would be the last time she saw her son alive, Merry didn't even notice Harold leave until he held out a damp cloth in front of her.

"Sorry doesn't even begin to cover it, honey. You know I didn't mean to..."

Merry heard the hitch of tears in Harold's voice before it trailed off. She took the hand towel and held it against her face. "Hit me? Yeah, I know. It's much worse than that, Harold. You were going to strike our child. This? I can forgive this," she muttered, spitting out a mouthful of blood, "but you were going to hurt Joshua. That I won't forgive. Ever. He hurts himself enough. He doesn't need anything from you except support and love. A fist in his face won't solve a damn thing."

"I do love him, but I won't condone what he's doing to himself. What he's done to our family. Won't have it in my house."

Merry faced her spouse of nearly twenty-three years, her eyes blazing with anger. "You mean our house. And I won't have my son living on the streets because you can't handle his medical issues."

"Medical issues? Oh please, not that again, Merry! He's just a headstrong kid who wants the party life rather than real life!"

"He's an addict, Harold. Heroin is one of the hardest habits to overcome! He needs to detox, stick with counseling, and be part of a supportive environment…"

Harold threw his hands in the air in frustration. "No, what he needs is…"

Merry lost it. "I've had enough of you telling me what he needs because you don't have a clue! Hell, even I'm at loss at this point. What I do know—what I feel in my heart—is Joshua needs to know we will always be here for him, no matter what. Because the world he's in now will destroy him. You may have given up on him, but I certainly haven't. He's not a broken toy you can just discard, Harold. He's our son."

Merry threw the blood-soaked towel on the porch and went back inside. Snatching her purse and keys from the kitchen counter, she raced back to the front door. Harold stood in the same spot, unmoving, staring down the dark street. Moving past him, she took the stairs two at a time.

"Where are you going?"

Over her shoulder Merry yelled, "To find our son and bring him home. Try to stop me, and you'll find yourself single."

❖❖❖

It took Merry several attempts to open her eyes while she clawed her way up to awareness. The medication had finally kicked in and alleviated the stabbing pain inside her head, but it left her motor skills on the fritz.

The heartbreaking memories of the night Joshua left home and she went after him made tears roll down her cheeks. She wanted to erase the images of finding him hours later, incoherent, curled up in the fetal position on the porch of a drug den, a needle still in his arm.

"No! Please, I don't want to think about those times! Why can't I recall the good ones?"

Her answer was a lone whine, followed by a wet tongue on her arm.

"Oh shit! You scared the crap out of me, Percy! I forgot you were here. Gee, thanks for not munching on me while I was out."

Though still a bit groggy, Merry forced her muscles to work. She sat up, her back against the cabinet. Judging by the amount of sun streaming through the kitchen window, she'd been out for a while. She looked at the microwave for confirmation, and sure enough, it was almost eleven a.m.

They are coming faster and lasting longer. This one was bad. I was out for almost three full hours! Guess it didn't help Mookie smacked me around. Oh well, he certainly won't be doing that again to me...or anyone else. Fucker.

Percy was right next to her, tail thumping, snout inches from her leg. His focus never shifted from Merry's face. "If I didn't know any better, I'd swear you look worried." She reached out to pet him. "Be glad you're a dog and don't get migraines. The pain is beyond excruciating. Makes you want to blow your brains out."

Percy's long, unkempt nails scratched on the linoleum when he scooted closer. After one more lick, he rested his head on her thigh and snorted out a burst of air. Merry glanced over to the broken bowl and uneaten tuna on the floor, surprised Percy left it untouched. He had to be hungry.

"Okay, so I failed at dog ownership 101. Tuna is for cats, not canines. I don't really have anything else here yet, so I'll need to go shopping. I've got some other items to buy besides dog kibble—plus I need to clean out my car—so it might take me a while. Come on. Let me show you where you'll be staying until I get back."

Percy followed her like he'd been by her side his entire life. They trudged through the high grass, out past the pond, and over to the old barn that was nearly two full acres from the house. The old building was completely hidden from view by an overgrown section of pine and magnolia trees. The barn had four stalls and a hayloft. Merry went over to the first stall and peeked inside. There was an old water trough. In the corner by the steps leading up to the loft, there was an old hose attached to a spigot. She smiled, glad she'd had the utilities turned on the week prior. In minutes, Percy had fresh water.

She considered locking him up in the stall, but couldn't bring herself to confine him in such a small area. Walking the perimeter, she made sure there were no holes or missing sections of wood.

Percy scoped out the place via his nose. Kneeling down, she called to him, and he trotted through the dust to her side.

"For now, at least temporarily, this will be your new home while I'm gone. Wasn't planning on being here until Saturday, but that's changed now. So, let me get some things we'll both need, and then I'll be back."

Percy nudged his moist nose against her forehead. As Merry petted him, she felt a lump underneath his neck. Inspecting it closer, she realized it was a scar. Percy whined and pulled his head away. Suddenly, she realized why she'd never heard him bark. "That bastard! Rest assured, while I'm still alive, your life will never consist of pain or violence again. That's a promise. Enjoy exploring your surroundings. I've got to go. Be back soon."

Percy's gaze shifted when the sound of something scurrying in the farthest stall caught his attention. She used the moment to leave, shutting the heavy door behind her.

After retrieving her keys, she went to the car. She gathered up the ruined towels and walked out back, tossing them into the old, rusty drum used to burn garbage. Once back at her car, she gunned the engine and took off, eager to get to her other house to shower and change before she went shopping for supplies.

14

New cell phone acquired and trunk packed with groceries and clothes, Merry headed out to the farm. She already knew cell reception was terrible at the new place, so she decided to make a few phone calls while she still had service. Waffling back and forth over whether she should call Deb or Derek, she settled on Deb, since she hadn't returned her calls from the other day.

On the second ring, Deb answered. "Well it's about time! I've only called you like twenty times!"

"Sorry. I dropped my phone in a sink full of water the other day. Tried to let it dry it out a couple of days in a bag of rice, but it was a dead horse. Had to suck it up and buy another one today."

"See? That's why you have a dishwasher! Washing plates by hand went out of style decades ago. What's wrong with yours?"

Exiting the main highway, Merry responded, "Nothing is wrong with my dishwasher. Unlike you, I like to pre-rinse."

Debbie snorted. "Waste of time and bad for the manicure.

Enough about that topic. Glad you're accessible again because I've missed talking to you. How's your vacation?"

Oh, just fine! Killed two people in less than three days, and acquired a new dog! Yours?

"My forced time off has been a blast. Really. I mean, things can't get any better."

Debbie burst out laughing. "My bestie—always the comedienne. If you're bored, you should come hang with me. Our favorite zombie show has a new episode tonight. Oh, better yet! Want me to come over and help you finish packing so things will go smoother on Saturday? We've got five hours until show time. I'll even bring dinner."

"You are sweet to offer, but I'll pass. I'm actually on my way to the new place right now with a load of items. Wanted to start trying to settle in a bit at a time, you know, before I'm forced at once?"

Debbie softened her tone. "That's a good idea, sweetie. This is going to be a major transition for you, and breaking it down into manageable pieces is probably best. Are you going to spend the night, too?"

"Yep. It'll be strange for sure, but I'll manage."

"Of course you will, dear. If you get freaked out, just call Derek. Or me. You know we're always here for you. Always."

"Yes, I know, even though both of you sometimes are a tad overzealous. As I've mentioned numerous times, I'm a big girl. I can take care of myself."

"The bigger the girl, the larger the shoulders needed to cry on. Mine, along with my ass, are huge. Okay, so now that we've gotten all that out of the way, I've gotta ask you...Did you put in a good word for me the other night?"

"I tried, but I'm afraid it didn't help. Derek will always see you like he does me—a little sister. You're on your own, girl. Maybe wear something clingy and sheer on Saturday. He does think you're gorgeous, funny, and smart. His words, not mine. So, you're going to have to approach this in a different way. I'll let you figure exactly how on your own. Fair?"

Debbie squealed so loud Merry held the phone away from

her ear. "Yes! That's a start! Thanks for telling me. You just made my evening!"

The phone beeped with an incoming call. Merry stiffened when she saw it was from Derek. "Speaking of your quarry, that's him. Let me call you back."

Merry didn't wait for a response from Debbie. Instead, she swapped calls. "Hey, bro! Done playing detective for the weekend?"

There was a long pause before Derek spoke. "Nope. The job's like herpes: it never really disappears, only hibernates for a while."

Merry sensed the unease in his voice and figured Mookie's remains must have been discovered. She had to force herself to not sound giddy. "Derek...what's wrong? And don't tell me 'nothing' because I hear it in your voice."

Ignoring the question, Derek prodded. "Where are you?"

Yep, he knows. Shit! Did I leave something behind, and he's going to interrogate me? Maybe someone saw me running with Percy?

"Driving. Unfortunately, there was a tragic cell phone accident that didn't get fixed until today. Spent most of the weekend moving small things, you know, so Saturday won't take so long? So, if I missed a call from you before, I'm sorry."

"We need to talk. No, I need to talk. In person and not on the phone. I'll meet you at your place."

The bruises on her face would take days to heal. Sunglasses only hid so much, and she couldn't get away with wearing them while inside. She had to convince Derek to wait. Merry forced her voice to remain calm. "Can't it wait until tomorrow, or you just tell me now? I'm dancing close to a raging migraine. Planned on taking my meds and conking out early."

"No, it can't."

"Did you piss off your captain again? Don't tell me you got suspended for letting your temper get the upper hand over your mouth?"

Derek grunted. "Seriously, Sis. We need to talk. It can't wait, so I'm coming over. Be there in thirty."

"Derek, please? Not today. I don't feel very well and just want to rest. It's been a really long weekend."

Silence.

"Derek? You there?"

Dead air.

Glancing at her phone, noticing she had no service, Merry ground her teeth. She dropped the phone into her lap, made sure no one was around, and did a u-turn. Even if she could, it wouldn't do any good to call him back and beg. She heard it in his voice—the determination and wariness—and it sent chills up her spine. She could probably make it back home in twenty, so she had a brief window of opportunity to get things in order before he arrived.

A killer's life is never dull! Sorry, Percy. Dinner's going to be late.

***

Bursting through the front door, Merry made a beeline for the bathroom. After washing her face, she covered the dark bruises the best she could with concealer. Thankfully, it was on the right side of her face, so she let her hair down. With a good finger-tousle and head flip, along with a generous shot of spray, it cascaded just right to help aide in the concealment.

Stepping back, she gave her face a good once-over and then scowled. Though the makeup and strategic hair placement helped, the knot and discoloration were still visible. In the reflection, she noticed her knuckles still looked ugly, and traces of the tattoo remained on her arm.

As she scrubbed the last remnants of the tat from her bicep, she forced herself to calm down. She knew Derek would notice her injuries, yet maybe they could easily be explained. He knew she worked out like crazy, so if he asked, she'd simply tell him a partial truth and a blatant lie.

She attacked the bag without her gloves on, which made her skin crack and bleed. She'd been upset when she started, hadn't eaten anything, and overextended herself. Got dizzy and fainted on the garage floor, which left her with an ugly lump and a shiner. If he questioned her story, or seemed at all hesitant about believing it, Merry would take him to the garage. Show him the punching bag and the streaks of red.

That should shut him up! At least until I'm finished with my projects. Still can't believe Tad Tompkins is involved.

Merry made her way to the kitchen to fix a cold glass of tea for them both. When she passed the living room, she noticed the remnants of her old cell strewn across the hardwood. It took her a full minute to gather all the broken pieces up and toss them into the garbage. Then, she grabbed the tea and fixed two drinks. No sooner had she filled the tumblers with ice, Derek knocked once and then opened the front door.

"Merry?" Derek shouted while ambling up the stairs.

She closed her eyes and took a deep, relaxing breath. *You can do this.*

"In the kitchen. Just made some tea and took my pill. My advice is to hurry up and tell me what's going on before I zone out. Can't promise how long I'll be awake."

"Shouldn't leave your doors unlocked, Sis," Derek muttered walking into the kitchen. "It's dangerous. Wow, you've been a busy gal. Not much left for us to move on...yikes! What happened to your face and hands?"

Merry tried to keep her tone normal, steady. It didn't work. She heard the edginess in her voice and internally cringed at the words. "Looks worse than it really is. Getting older makes injuries seem bigger. Uglier. Oh, and age also brings balance issues front and center. Discovered the hard way that when you jab and punch without gloves on, you bleed. Step in said blood, you fall. Hard. Enough about me. You wanted to come over here and talk about something important, so spill."

A scowl crossed Derek's face. "You've always been such a hardhead. Serves you right for trying to act like you're twenty. I'm serious about your doors, though. In today's world, you can't be too careful, especially when you live alone. Just because you're all rough and buff now doesn't mean you'd be immune to hot lead."

Merry sensed his dark mood. Saw the creases of worry and lack of sleep etched deep across her brother's brow and around his eyes. She handed him a glass of tea and made her way into the living room. Settling on the sofa, she remarked, "Oops. Told you my head is thumping, and you know how I get when it morphs into a full-blown attack. Again, enough about me. To quote you the other day, you look like hell. What's so damned important it couldn't wait until my head didn't feel like it was going to explode? Zombie apocalypse start or something?"

Derek sat in the chair across from Merry, his gaze sweeping over her face and arms. She couldn't tell if he bought her story or not. "For some."

Merry cocked her head with feigned curiosity. "What, did you guys get your first case of a user on bath salts here? Is that what's freaked you out? Seriously, bro, you look like you've seen a ghost. Or a real zombie."

"Case I assisted on today was rough. Vic was one of Mitch's, and the second drug dealer in two days to bite the big one. The guy's face and neck were gone, though not from a zombie or a crazy on salts. His dog munched on him. I probably won't be able to eat for a week after seeing that up close and personal. Made me really grateful Stonewall is a toy Pom and that I don't work homicide."

Merry's heart skipped a beat. *He went to the scene? Why? Figures Mitch is Mookie's handler! Justice gods 2: Murphy's Law 1.*

"How awful! Just the thought makes me nauseated. You said second dealer. Do you all think there's a connection to Peppy's death?"

"At first glance, no. Looked like a simple case of a bad owner got his comeuppance. Once the scene was processed and no signs of forced entry were found, and vic's cell phone is missing, the consensus is another hit. Mitch is all up in arms about the whole thing. Never seen him so wound up."

Merry bit her lip, holding back the numerous questions on the tip of her tongue. She didn't want to seem too eager or interested in the particulars, so she switched gears. "You rarely discuss work, Derek. A trick I think you learned from Dad. The crime scene must have been extra gruesome if you want to talk. Somehow, I don't get the sense that's the only thing bothering you, so talk. Again, not sure how much longer I have." Merry forced a yawn. "But I'm all ears now."

Derek kept his eyes on the glass, unwilling to look up. Uncomfortable silence filled the house for almost a full minute before he spoke again. "You know, there's a reason I don't work homicide. I can't stand looking at all the nastiness that happens when people die. Saw my share of carnage and blood when I worked the streets. Still have nightmares about some of the accident scenes I worked. Dad warned me about those things when I told him I wanted to go to the academy. Said he saw his share of cops become either raging drunks or eat their guns because some memories don't disappear. I became a cop because I wanted to make a difference in my little section of the world. Sometimes, I believe I made the wrong choice. Should have just gone on to medical school after I got my biology degree. Days like today give me serious pause about my career decision and make me contemplate turning in my badge."

"Oh, Derek, stop talking like that! You make a difference every day! You, Mitch, your entire squad. All of you put your lives on the line each time you step out the front door!"

"Grow up, Merry. Stop fooling yourself. Our unit barely makes a dent in comparison to what's really on the streets."

"That's not true, Derek."

"Our Captain disagrees. In fact, Mitch and I were grilled for over two hours today about the issue, among other things. The entire incident left a sour taste in my mouth."

"Maybe you're the one who needs a vacation. Hasn't it been over two years since your last visit to Miami?"

"Next month will be three."

"See there! It's only been one year since all of us went to..." Merry felt a strong pang of sadness hit her chest at the memory of the last family vacation in Branson. It took her a second to refocus. "You insisted I needed a break, and the time since my last one has been much shorter for me. Heed your own advice. Take a leave of absence. If you prefer, I could just go talk to your captain and insist. Tell him how worried I am about you and your mental state. Maybe he'll be as understanding as Judge Tompkins was."

Derek rolled his eyes. "You aren't ever going to let me live that down, are you?"

"Nope. Rather annoying having someone poke their nose into your business...agree?"

"Okay, I get it." Derek sighed. "I love you; you love me. We both worry too much about each other."

"So, does that mean you are going to follow through and take some time off? I'm not the only one who's suffered losses in the last six months. I think each of us need some time to heal. Regroup. What did Dad used to say? Yank on our grown-up panties?"

Derek's laugh was bitter. "Yeah, that's the phrase."

Merry set her glass down on the coffee table and scrutinized Derek's body language. He looked beyond tired. Deflated and exhausted were better descriptions. "When you said 'other things' what did you mean?" Merry knew she was on to something the second the words left her lips. She could see Derek tense up.

"My entire unit was questioned about not only our whereabouts the last forty-eight hours but also our commitment to the department. Captain didn't come right out and accuse anyone of impropriety, but the subtle hints were there. Seems not only Hudson thinks something is fishy about the deaths of two snitches so close together. According to Mitch, Hudson accused him of taking out his charges. Said things were too clean, not done by some street thug or enemy. Hinted he didn't think a pro was behind things either. Hudson—and others—thinks it's a cop. Didn't help any that someone fitting Mitch's general description was seen talking to the vic only hours before he died and that person drove a motorcycle. I had to get in between Mitch and Hudson at the scene when Hudson made a snide remark about Mitch owning a bike. There's so much suspicion floating around the department right now. Everyone is walking on eggshells. The job is stressful enough without all this added bullshit. "

Great. Just great.

"You're serious about quitting the force, aren't you?"

Derek bit his lip and nodded. Merry noticed a deep sadness

behind his eyes. She stood and walked over and knelt down in front of him.

"If your heart is telling you it's had enough, then listen. You've had almost twenty amazing years on the job. Made your contribution to society in one way, so why not try another? Science was always your first love, so maybe you should consider that avenue. I...don't like seeing you like this, Derek. In fact, I've never seen you so distraught before. Our family...we've been through a lot. First losing Mom in such a tragic way, then Dad's slow and agonizing death, then, well, you know. Sometimes, tragedy shifts the direction of our lives in ways we never imagined."

Derek looked away from Merry's intense gaze. "It'll be hard to start over. Being a cop is all I know. But I gotta say, I'm sick of all the lies. Tired of walking the thin line of living two separate lives. Add in this latest twist of never-ending suspicion and it's just too much to handle. In short, I'm burned out."

"The question is, dear brother, is being a cop what defines you? If it is, then you need to sit back and really take stock of yourself. Because at the end of the day, it's just a job. Derek Isaac Clarke is an amazing man who happens to work as a police officer. He would be the same amazing guy if he bagged groceries or sold auto parts. Plain and simple."

"Dad would be so disappointed..." Derek whispered, his voice trailing off.

"He would not! Besides, even if he was here and said to your face he was, that shouldn't stop you. It's your life, after all. You live it, and the rest of us don't. Now, quit being such a big wimp and follow what you know to be the right course for your life. That's exactly what I've done. Debbie thinks I'm nuts for selling this place and moving so far away from work..."

"So do I."

Merry stood and cocked her head in defiance. "Okay, so you both think I'm crazy. Your opinions didn't stop me from making decisions and choices contrary to yours, now did it?"

"No."

"Well, there you go. End of discussion. Now please, before I fall asleep standing up..."

Derek rose and hugged Merry tight. "I know; I know. You need to rest. Sorry for keeping you so long, but I needed to vent. Thanks. Love you."

"Love you, too," Merry replied into Derek's shoulder. "I'll be in and out the next few days, moving a few more items, so cell service will be sketchy."

Derek pulled away and headed downstairs. "And I'll be busy trying to decide what new job title I should strive for, so no worries. See you Saturday. Oh, and one more thing."

"What's that?"

Derek paused by the front door, a stern look on his face. "The next time you decide to beat the shit out of the bag, eat first, and remember to wear gloves. Black and blue are not good colors on you."

Merry gave Derek a weak smile and watched him walk out the door. The lump of hot tears formed fast in her throat, surprising her with their appearance. The salty mess was a mixture of guilt for putting Derek in the middle of her plans and sadness at the knowledge the heart-to-heart chat was the final one they'd have inside the house.

Yet the thing that made the tears race down her cheeks was how proud she was of Derek for recognizing he needed a change and doing something about it. Unlike their father, who resolved himself to the life until he retired, unhappy and frustrated with the profession he'd chosen. Even on his deathbed, their father wouldn't let go of the anger and bitterness.

Proud of you, big brother. You'll need something new to occupy your thoughts soon.

15

"Don't give me that look! You wouldn't enjoy the trip anyway. Sitting in a car for hours watching someone isn't much fun. Besides, my cover would be blown if I had to let you out to do your business. You're just going to have to hang here until I get back."

Percy whined, thumping his tail against the floor. His big, dark eyes seemed to plead for Merry to change her mind. Ever since she'd returned on Sunday, Percy had been glued to her side. Housetraining turned out to be a breeze. All she had to do was get up and go outside and walk around to the back of the barn every few hours. Percy followed, and when the call of nature hit, he did his thing and then came right back.

The poor creature had been so starved for attention, he couldn't get enough. She'd tripped over him several times because Percy insisted on being right next to her—even when she was in the bathroom. Twice, while Merry went through Peppy's cell records, hoping she might find some contact with

Tad, Percy fell asleep against her leg. She'd almost forgotten he was there until he made water leak from her eyes with a noxious, invisible cloud. In the back of her mind was a mental note to switch dog food brands the next time she went shopping.

A bolt of lightning flashed, followed by a clap of thunder so loud the entire house shook. Percy cowered next to Merry's leg. She glanced out the front window, cringing at the gun-metal gray clouds swirling overhead.

Though it was risky, she couldn't force herself to lock Percy inside the barn. She'd made a promise not to hurt or mistreat him while in her care. Leaving him inside the house wasn't an option either. It wasn't that she worried about him having an accident but more about the slight chance of a surprise visit from Deb or Derek. There would be no way to explain Percy's presence, especially to Derek.

Considering her mission was to simply watch and observe Tad, Merry made her decision. Grabbing her purse and keys from the counter, she walked outside and headed to the car. She didn't need a leash or to even tell the dog to come or get inside the car.

"I certainly never intended to have a partner-in-crime. At least I know you'll never rat me out. Must say, it is nice having a chance to vocalize my thoughts. Kind of hard to keep things straight sometimes. So, thanks Percy. I appreciate you listening to my ramblings."

❊❊❊

The heavy rain in the outskirts of the county had morphed into a light, sporadic drizzle inside the city limits. Percy was curled up on the floorboard, lulled to sleep from the car ride. Merry drove down Chester Street, looking for a silver Tahoe. She spotted it in front of the fourth house on the right, along with Tad standing in the yard talking on his phone, his back toward the street. Continuing on, she made a loop through the neighborhood, making mental notes of the area. Once finished, she pulled into the parking lot of an abandoned convenience store at the end of the street and smiled at the perfect view of Tad's driveway.

Cracking the windows, Merry shut the engine off. She scanned the area, making sure she was alone. This part of Little Rock was older, the tracts of land larger than the newer subdivisions but the houses smaller in size. Most of the residents were elderly with only a smattering of families with small children. Merry recalled an argument between father and son in the judge's chambers the day Tad stopped by to announce he'd purchased the place. Judge Tompkins tried to convince a headstrong Tad the decision was foolish and didn't comprehend why in the world his son would pick that particular part of town to live in. The judge said resale value in the area was low and tried to change Tad's mind. Son told father to shut up, he was no longer a child and didn't need his approval. Merry remembered being inside her office, shaking her head at Tad's upstart demeanor and total lack of respect for his father and silently agreeing with her boss's arguments.

Considering what he did for a living, the choice Tad opted to call home made perfect sense. Houses were far enough apart from each other one couldn't overhear conversations, and nosey neighbors went to sleep early.

Smart boy.

Merry grabbed the binoculars from the seat and focused them on Tad's house. She cringed when she noticed cameras by the front and garage doors. Though not surprising, their presence did complicate matters. It's not like she could just lure Tad out of the house with a fake phone call, pretending to be a junkie in need of a fix, since she didn't have his number.

Tad paced around in his yard, and the cameras hadn't moved. Merry hoped that meant they were stationary, which would make sneaking up from a different angle to spray them with paint easier. If not, she'd just have to be extra careful and camouflaged when it came time to take the bastard out.

Tad Tompkins was in his early thirties. and he rarely spoke to his father. She knew Tad was a constant source of disappointment for Judge Tompkins. Any time Tad's name was mentioned, she could see it in his face. Merry tried to recall a recent conversation about the boy but came up blank.

The relationship started to sour less than a month after

Merry started working at the courthouse. Judge Tompkins's wife, Rachel, died in his arms of a massive heart attack a week before her sixtieth birthday. The entire staff went to the funeral, and it was Merry's first interaction with Tad. She remembered the shock and anger she felt at the boy for the lack of not only grief at the loss of his mother but concern or compassion toward his destroyed father.

Tad had been an obnoxious, barely twenty-something back when his mother passed away. He'd been home only three weeks after getting kicked out of college for cheating when she died. At the time, Merry chalked up his behavior to his age and inability to express his emotions from the loss of his mother. It wasn't until she witnessed several interactions with his father that Merry came to realize Tad Tompkins was nothing more than a spoiled, rich brat with no heart or consideration for anyone other than himself.

The thin tendril of family ties frayed even more when Tad was arrested several years later and charged with DUI. Judge Tompkins had been mortified by Tad's actions. He stood firm and made Tad pay for his mistake, insisting he be shown no special treatment. She remembered going home that night and telling Harold about the situation, each commenting on how awful it would be to be faced with such a decision.

It wasn't long after they found out exactly how hard it was to have that particular problem.

Digging deeper into her memories, she seemed to recall Tad worked with computers. The official word was he designed websites and specialized in graphics. A fleeting conversation with Debbie in the kitchen one day years ago popped up. On a whim, Debbie decided to try her hand at selling some overpriced cosmetics and needed a website. Judge Tompkins recommended Tad, and to appease her boss, Debbie gave it a shot. Two days—and one very pissed off customer later—Debbie swore she would never recommend Tad for anything other than a swift kick in the groin.

"He showed up and seemed normal for about five minutes. When I brought my laptop out to show him the homepage of the cosmetics company, he tried to kiss me! I mean, one second he's sitting across the table, and the next, he's in my face, his tongue flopping like a wet worm! Can you believe it? When I told him I wasn't interested, and it was time for him to leave, he actually tried to smooth things over by offering me a joint. Said I needed to smoke some and relax, and then he'd show me a good time. Ugh! I'd never been so happy to see my husband drive up! I swear, the guy is beyond creepy!"

Merry had pressed Debbie to tell their boss what happened, but Debbie refused. Said she didn't want to get on the bad side of the judge by basically calling his son a pervert and a pothead. It wasn't long after the incident with Debbie that Tad was arrested. Merry and Debbie thought it just punishment.

And now here I am, sitting in the dark and watching the little pervert who's not just some geeky nerd fond of weed. Tad's a major drug player in Central Arkansas. A heroin dealer! Does his father have a clue? An inkling...a little tickle in the back of his mind? No, no way. If he knew, he wouldn't stand for it.

Pulling up old childhood memories, Merry thought about the friendship between her father and the judge. Back then, he was simply Ronald Arthur Tompkins. A beat cop paired up with her dad, working the streets of Little Rock, and a frequent guest at their house for dinner. The tight-knit union began to unravel when Officer Tompkins decided to become an attorney and quit the force to attend law school. According to conversations she overheard late at night between her mom and dad, her father felt betrayed by his closest friend. There was a distinct line between law and order, and the majority of law enforcement considered attorneys nothing more than rats in three-piece suits, tearing apart all the dangerous and hard work by the police.

The two friends drifted apart and the fun-filled visits by "Uncle Ron" ceased. Merry didn't see him again until her mother's funeral, and it was only a brief glimpse. The funeral was over, and Merry was sandwiched between Derek and her dad as they made their way to the black limo. Merry didn't understand at the time why Derek wouldn't let her say hello. Instead, Derek forced her inside the car while her father veered off to talk to his former friend. Though she couldn't hear what was being said between them, she could tell her father's words were not friendly. The interaction lasted less than a minute, and she didn't see her former "uncle" again until she applied for the trial court assistant position with the county. When she came in to interview, she'd been shocked to discover the job was with Judge Tompkins.

Since her father had passed away, Merry decided whatever beef the two men had was their problem, not hers. Derek, on the other hand, didn't feel the same way. The bonds of the blue ran just as deep as blood ties, and he tried to convince her not to take the job.

"What do you think Dad would say?" Derek had prodded.

"I'm sure something I wouldn't like and would just ignore. This isn't the old days any longer, Derek. Law and order work together as a cohesive unit now, remember? The days of their side and our side are over. Besides, I need the job. The pay is fantastic, it will give me something to occupy by days with now that Joshua is in school, and the retirement package is phenomenal. In other words, butt out of my business."

Derek had stormed out of the house and didn't speak to her for an entire month. Eventually, he got used to the idea, and though he never apologized for being an overbearing ass, he did learn to deal with it and never said another word.

In the dark, Merry snorted at the twisted irony. Two friends separated because of archaic ideas about the justice system would now have the common thread of the cop's daughter killing the judge's son.

Twilight Zone shit. Daddy, I miss you, yet I'm glad you aren't here to see what I've become. I know you'd try to stop me or insist I seek counseling or medical help to cope with everything. The thing is, I did all that before and it didn't work. The only thing keeping me alive now is the drive to kill and right the wrongs done to my family. I hope, if you and Mom are in some other dimension and can hear me, you will be able to forgive me for what I've done.

She thought about what Mookie said about Tad. How he had connections and money to keep them out of prison. Those connections didn't seem to keep Mookie from getting arrested numerous times, although he never received more than a fine and time served in county lockup. His response about his handler—and the rock-drop in her gut—told her it was Mitch. Thought back to how Mookie acted when she first started questioning him, assuming she was a cop.

The last several days Merry went over every word Mookie had said. What was really behind his comment about not saying shit to the cops when busted the night before about the next shipment? After mulling over the conversation for hours, the picture her mind created was not one she wanted to see. It boiled down to two possible scenarios, both of which made her feel sick to her stomach.

A dirty cop or bought-and-paid for judge.

Merry didn't know Mitch like she did Judge Tompkins. If forced to choose a side, she had no doubts she'd pick Mitch for the dirty one. She wasn't so naïve to think a judge couldn't be a part of a drug ring, for God knows Arkansas had seen its share of trusted, public figures crash and burn when their true colors emerged. From corrupt governors to lying medical examiners, all the way to a prosecutor or two indicted by the Feds under RICO statutes, even to the rumors of the Mena airport used for a drug drop in the 80s, Arkansas was a haven for narcotics.

So it was among the realm of possibilities Judge Tompkins not only knew, but even funded, his son's illicit activities. After all, he was human, and people made mistakes. However, Merry had worked by his side for years and had never seen him act in any way, shape, or form one could even consider inappropriate. He followed the letter of the law and handed down his rulings with such precision, not one of his cases had ever been overturned on appeal.

Mitch was a different story. The first time she met him, Merry's impression wasn't favorable. Mitch was brash, cocky, beyond confident in his looks and seduction skills. Arrogance exuded from him like cheap cologne on a hot day. She'd disliked him from the start, and not just because Mitch was an overbearing asshole. She sensed the darkness underneath the façade of burly cop. Though she'd only seen it a few times—the most recent at Joshua's funeral—there was sense of malevolence behind his eyes.

Hmmm, now I know why.

The sparkle of red taillights yanked her back to the present. The Tahoe backed out onto the street and headed her way. Merry slunk down in the seat and waited until she heard the SUV pass by before sitting back up. Her movements woke Percy up. He stretched and jumped into the passenger seat.

Merry started the car but didn't turn the headlights on while she eased out of the parking lot. "You sleep through the boring part and wake up just in time for some fun. Typical male."

***

It was after three a.m. when Merry turned down the long dirt road leading to the new house. Even though it was late, she was amped up after a successful first night of stalking. In just one evening, she learned some interesting habits exhibited by Tad. He'd hit six clubs in less than four hours, staying at each one only long enough to make a few quick sales and then skip out before anyone really noticed he'd been there.

She couldn't help but wonder if Tad's actions were part of his normal behavior or newly acquired because of the loss of two of his dealers.

"Come on, boy. I don't know about you, but I'm starved. Let's have a little snack, okay?"

Percy licked his lips and followed Merry along the dark walkway. The only sound besides their movement across the yard was the rhythmic cadence of the katydids. Once inside the kitchen, Merry poured a cupful of nuggets into Percy's bowl. While he chomped away, she grabbed a protein bar and bottle of water from the fridge. After taking her shoes off and grabbing her cell from the counter, she walked out to the back porch and sat at the small table.

She powered on her cell and waited for the screen to come on, more out of habit rather than anything else. Other than Debbie or Derek, there really wasn't anyone left to contact her. She'd mailed Steve the copy of Harold's death certificate two days before. Savannah had dropped her little emotional bombshell by already. The papers were signed and closing completed on both houses. Calls from distant relatives and acquaintances, expressing their condolences through the phone lines, stopped months ago.

So Merry was surprised when she had a missed call and a voicemail from a number she didn't recognize—until it was too late. The computer-generated voice made her skin crawl.

"Mrs. Hall, this is Dr. Cash's office. Please contact our office to schedule a follow-up appointment as soon as possible. Our records indicate your prescription expires next month and will not be renewed until a full examination is completed. Thank you."

"Not going to happen," Merry whispered to the still night air.

Merry pushed the call from her thoughts like it had never happened. It was time to let her sick mind run amuck plotting out the end of Tad Tompkins and figure out just who in the hell was the next rung on the ladder. She hoped and prayed she was wrong on both counts, and her quarry would be yet another stranger.

Not someone she knew.

The only way to find out for sure was to make Tad talk and not kill him before she drained every bit of information from his head.

Percy nudged his moist nose against Merry's thigh. She reached out and patted his back. The irritation she felt at the entire debacle the night at Mookie's was gone, replaced by the warmth of companionship with her new furry housemate.

"You were worth it, buddy."

16

10:00 A.M. SATURDAY MORNING

Debbie arrived at the house first, hair piled on top of her head, a few ringlets framing her face. Her ample curves were strategically on display in Lycra shorts and a workout top so tight Merry wondered how she could breathe.

"I see you took my suggestion to wear something clingy today to a whole new level! You do realize when you bend over to pick up a box or something your girls are going to..."

"Be front and center for Derek to ogle? Of course I do! What good is it to have to wag these heavy things around if I can't use them to bend men to my will?"

Merry laughed. "I'll be lucky if Derek doesn't fall and break something today while he's busy drooling over you. If he damages any of my furniture, I'm holding you responsible."

Debbie waved her hand in the air, dismissing Merry's words with a flick of her wrist. "A price I'm more than willing to pay for a chance to have a night with...oh, wow! It really looks different in here! You weren't kidding when you said you'd moved a bunch of stuff, were you?"

"Nope. If you recall, I had nothing better to do during the last seven days."

Debbie rolled her eyes. "Whatever. So, what time is my sexy cop showing up with the moving van?"

"Any minute now, so you'll just have to do with me until he arrives."

Merry stiffened at the sound of Mitch's voice.

What the hell is he doing here?

Instead of being embarrassed by the comment, Debbie beamed and turned her attention to the doorway. She did her best impression of a sexy Southern Belle. "Why Mitchell Sinclair! I do declare you are just too adorable for words! How very gallant of you to offer your brawn to help us little gals today. You just proved chivalry isn't dead."

Merry forced her voice to remain neutral. She watched Mitch saunter up the stairs, expecting his gaze to be trained on Debbie's cleavage. She was surprised to see he wasn't even looking in Debbie's direction. His intense gaze was on Merry. Returning the stare, she grumbled, "Mitch. I wasn't aware you were coming today."

"Hope you don't mind I invited myself, Merry. Derek mentioned the other day he was helping you move, and I had some free time, so..."

Merry ground her teeth. "So here you are. How wonderful."

Debbie shot a confused glance over to Merry, stunned by the cold tone. "I think it's great you're here to help. The more hands on deck the better."

Mitch was at the top of the staircase, a devious grin on his full lips. Merry watched his gaze shift from her eyes to Debbie's body. He looked at Debbie like she was dessert. "Well at least someone appreciates my presence today."

Debbie waved Mitch's comment off and hugged him. "Both of us do. This is just going to be a difficult day, so cut her some slack, okay?"

Merry held in her snide comments as Derek bounded up the steps. "Geez, not one bead of sweat dripping yet and I already hear bickering? This should be an interesting day. Hey, Mitch! Thanks for the help. See there? You ladies can simply point and direct and we'll handle the heavy work. Your nails are safe today."

I hate Murphy's Law.

❋ ❋ ❋

Two hours and countless trips up and down the stairs later, the house was completely empty. Mitch and Derek had taken the last item—the couch—out and Merry could hear them grunting and grumbling with each other about the best way to situate it inside the van. Debbie gave the mantle above the fireplace one last swipe with a damp cloth when Merry walked in from the kitchen with a mop and bucket.

"All shiny and ready for the new owners. So, is your real estate agent coming by to get the keys?"

Merry shook her head. "No. She asked me to leave them in the mailbox. She'll come by and get them today after the open house she's working is over. Said it would be around 12:30, so we best scoot before she shows up. The woman is nice enough but has a mouth that never shuts up."

Debbie walked across the living room and smiled. "Good idea. I don't think you're in the mood for idle chitchat today, judging by your silence the last two hours. You gonna be okay?"

Merry stared out the sliding glass window into the backyard. Her eyes settled on the sparkling blue water of the pool. Memories of watching Harold teach Joshua to swim years ago floated by. She remembered all the times Harold had scooped her into his arms and made love to her in just about every room of the house. The winter of 2000 when they were without power for three days, all three of them huddled up under blankets by the warm fire. She could almost still hear Joshua's laughter when Harold teased her about not being able to swim, or the numerous dinners she ruined after overcooking them.

God, this is harder than I thought it would be. I miss you both so much.

"Yep. Can't get on with my life until I let this chapter close. Even if I could have handled staying inside these walls full of memories, the place is simply too big for me to keep up with alone. Taking care of the pool requires a lot of time. Add in the yard and housework, well, it was just going to be too much. It was time to downsize."

Debbie looped her arm in Merry's. "I know I gave you shit before about the selling the place, and for that, I'm sorry. I was just worried you were making a rash decision. You know, not thinking straight due to grief? The more I thought about it, and tried to put myself in your shoes, I realized I was wrong. Though I'm still a bit concerned about your long commute each day, especially when the clocks fall back an hour and you're driving in the dark, I get it. From the pictures you showed me, it looks like your new home is really tranquil."

"It is. The only noise at night is from insects and random wildlife. Plus, the house is much smaller. Upkeep will be easier."

"Sis? You about ready?"

Merry watched Derek and Mitch amble up the stairs. Moving away from Debbie, she walked over to the doorframe and ran her hands over the smooth wood. Though she had promised to repaint it, she couldn't bring herself to cover up all the years she and Harold had marked Joshua's growth spurts in the wood.

I love you, baby.

Derek's warm hand touched Merry's shoulder. He gave it a gentle squeeze. "Why don't you let Debbie or Mitch drive your car and you ride with me?"

Merry took in a long breath, filling her memory banks up with the scents of her old life. "Driving will help calm my nerves. I'll just crank up the radio and sing my blues away."

"Dad always said you were as stubborn as a mule."

The four of them walked down the stairs in silence, Merry at the end of the line. She shut and locked the door for the final time in her life, leaving her emotions trapped inside the empty space.

When Merry turned down the long road toward her house, her heartbeat increased. The mental image of Percy running up to greet them set her nerves on fire. Though she hated herself for thinking it, she was glad at the moment Percy was unable to bark. His whine was low enough so it couldn't be heard inside the house. If somehow the noise did carry all the way to the house, the sound of a dog making noise in the country was easily explained.

Merry pulled wide and let Derek have the spot closest to the gate. Debbie rode with Derek in the rental truck. When she exited, the smile on her face announced to the world she was having a grand time.

If that outfit doesn't change Derek's mind, nothing will.

Mitch was the last to arrive. He parked his motorcycle next to the car and didn't say a word as he made his way over to the van. He nearly ran into the gatepost while watching Debbie jump up and down with excitement.

"Oh honey! The pictures you showed me didn't do the place justice at all. Look at those trees! They've got to be hundreds of years old! A wrap-around porch and a white picket fence? Yep, it's my idea of Heaven."

Debbie's exuberance made Merry smile. "Wait until you see the pond in the back. Clean clear water surrounded by weeping willows and a few magnolias. There's even a dock to fish from."

"Fish my ass. That's margarita central! Wow, it looks just like my nana's spread down in Sheridan, minus a barn! Remember all those summers our fingers were purple for days after shelling peas on her porch?"

"I think my pinky nail is still stained. Wait until you see inside. You'll really think you've stepped back in time. I swear the man who owned it before me didn't change a thing inside since 1960. Even the appliances are from the era."

Debbie threw her sweaty arms around Merry and hugged her tight. "This will be like a mini-vacation every time I come to visit you! A real trip down memory lane. Come on...I can't wait to see what it looks like inside."

"Let's get this stuff unloaded before the heat cranks up beyond one-hundred first. Then you two can gush about the interior. Hurry up before our hands are too slippery to carry anything."

Debbie's focus shifted from admiring the house to ogling Derek's biceps. "I just love a man who takes charge. Anything you say, Detective."

Merry watched a hint of red creep into Derek's cheeks. She turned and opened the gate, a sly grin on her lips.

There's hope yet, Deb. Keep working your mojo.

***

By four p.m., the van was empty and the house crammed full. Since the square footage was almost half of her other place, the rooms were quite a bit smaller, so her belongings took up every conceivable space. Merry stood in the entryway leading to the miniscule living room. Most of the decorations were superficial and boring. The place lacked the warmth and comfort of home because it looked like it had been staged. All of the pictures and mementoes of her life with Harold and Joshua were packed away, leaving the living area almost sterile.

Merry fought the urge to walk over and clock Mitchell upside the head. Even though he hadn't said much during the entire process, just his presence made her skin crawl. Knowing his dirty hands touched her furnishings made her almost physically ill.

From the kitchen, Debbie yelled, "Okay, boys! Who needs a beer?"

Swallowing the nasty responses on the tip of her tongue, Merry said nothing. She wanted to be alone, though understood suspicions would be aroused if she insisted everyone leave the second the last item was unpacked. Turning toward the kitchen, Merry heard both men respond in unison behind her. "Me!"

"Then come on out to the back porch, boys. While our new homeowner gave you two instructions on the proper placement of her things, I made an early dinner. I'm sure it's enough to refuel your empty tanks."

"If she didn't have eyes only for you, I'd be taking that home with me tonight. God, I could get lost in those mounds for hours. Still can't believe you haven't hit that yet."

Though the comment was meant to be heard only by the ears of Derek, Mitch's deep voice made it across the room and into Merry's. She'd kept her smart mouth in check long enough. Spinning around, she lit into Mitch. "Hit that?! Seriously, Mitch, you should have bought this place because the décor is from the era you seem stuck in. No wonder your wife left you and your relationships last about as long as the common cold!"

Mitch's face turned whiter than his shirt. Derek stared at her like she'd just spoken in Hebrew and announced she was an alien. Merry heard Debbie let out a small gasp from the kitchen. The tension in the house was heavier than the humidity outside, and just as uncomfortable.

"I was just..." Mitch stuttered.

"Don't even try, Mitchell. Nothing you say from this point forward will make up for that garbage you just spewed out."

Derek tried to intervene. "Merry! Calm down before you have an aneurysm or something. Your face is beet red!"

Ignoring her brother, Merry continued her tirade. "Thanks for dropping in—unannounced, mind you—and for helping Derek. It's time you leave before I really lose my temper. I won't have anyone talk that way about my friend—or any female for that matter—at least not in my presence. Whatever sick, twisted shit roaming around in your head spills out from that cesspool you call a mouth when you're alone is your business. In this house, it's mine. I won't have it. Period. Again, leave before I hit you with something."

Mitch never said a word. He gave a curt nod to Derek and left, unwilling to look Merry in the eye. Derek shot her an ugly look and followed his partner outside. Merry stood in the doorway, shaking as the adrenaline crash hit.

"I'm assuming I should say thank you for sticking up for my honor, though I have no idea what in the hell just happened."

Just a teaser of what I really wanted to say to the bastard.

The shakes hit hard and fast. Merry stumbled over to the couch and sat down. "What just happened was I let that egotistical knuckle-dragger know I won't tolerate his bullshit, warped views on sexuality and women. God, he's a Neanderthal."

Debbie leaned against the doorframe and crossed her arms. "Yeah? Well, we already knew that from years of being around him. Not falling for that, so try again."

Merry huffed. "I'm just sick of his mouth. Never have liked him, and being around his negativity today got to me. Must be the heat."

Derek tromped through the front door. He stopped in the middle of the living room and held his hands up in frustration. "What was that all about? Why did you let that stupid remark bother you so much? You know he didn't mean it."

"Stop sticking up for him, Derek. I realize he's your partner, but that doesn't excuse what he said. It was rude and demeaning, and again, I won't tolerate him treating Debbie like she's just a thing rather than a human being. Period."

"Thanks for trying to protect my honor but the defense wasn't necessary. I've had that boy's number for years. I can detect a dog when one comes sniffing around. Now, I won't let this day end on a sour note. Come on and eat. I didn't slave over a hot stove in this heat just to have it go to waste. Mitch is a big boy. He'll get over it."

Debbie turned and walked out to the back porch. Derek continued to stare at Merry, studying her face for an answer. She stood and shrugged her shoulders. "Stop looking at me like that. The bastard had it coming."

Derek didn't say a word in response. Merry moved past him and followed Debbie outside, Derek right on her heels.

Well, I wanted them to leave early. Bet they won't stay long after that little incident.

***

Delicious meal over and three beers each later, the atmosphere on the back porch lightened up. Merry didn't say much during dinner. She let Debbie take control of the conversation as she flirted and laughed with Derek. Instead, she stared out to the pond and recalled how she learned how to swim quite by accident in the pool at her old house.

It was late one night, a few weeks after Harold's funeral. Numbed by grief, she had decided to put an end to her suffering. Take herself out on her terms by jumping into the deep end of the pool. It would be over quick, and from what she'd read, drowning wasn't painful—just scary while one fought for air. Yet the minute her body went under, her will to live overpowered her limbs. When her feet touched the bottom, her muscles kicked in and forced her back to the surface.

It was at that precise moment the trajectory of her life shifted.

The alcohol left Merry pleasantly relaxed. She wasn't much of a drinker, only cracking a cold one maybe twice a year. One full bottle of 151-proof rum and the horrible hangover that lasted two-full days when she was a senior in high school wiped out her interest in booze.

"Sis? Did you hear me?"

Merry blinked twice and looked over at Derek. "Uh, no. Sorry. What did you say?"

Derek reached out and patted Merry's arm. "I asked if you wanted another beer."

"Oh, no. Think I've had my quota for the year. Do you really think you should have another before you go? I don't think getting a DWI will sit well with your captain."

Derek stood and laughed. "No, it certainly wouldn't. Don't worry about me because I'm done for the night. Thought you and Debbie might like another before we leave."

"I think we should probably call it a night, Derek. Let our gal here get some rest. We'll plan a housewarming party soon, once she gets her new nest all fluffed and ready."

Merry exchanged glances with Debbie, her eyes conveying gratitude.

"Okay. Well, let me use the facilities, and then I'll take you back to your car Deb."

Merry and Debbie remained silent until Derek was inside the house.

"You sure you're going to be okay? I can stay the night if you want some company."

"And mess up your chance of an amorous evening with my brother? No way. Look, I'm fine. Stop worrying so much about me. Judging by the way he's been fawning over you all afternoon, I'd say you need to concentrate on Derek, not me."

Debbie's cheeks and neck turned bright pink. "It's not just my imagination then, is it?"

Derek's heavy footsteps kept Merry from responding verbally. Instead, she smiled and shook her head. She gave Debbie a conspiratorial wink and stood. "Thanks again for all the help, but I really am beat. It'll take me a few days to get settled in, so how about lunch Thursday or Friday?"

"Sounds great."

Merry heard the coldness in Derek's voice. She turned around and found him standing at the back door, a strange look on his face. Grabbing her plate and glass, Merry made her way toward him, studying his rigid posture through her peripheral vision.

"Do you want some help with the dishes?" Debbie asked as they walked past Derek into the kitchen.

"You two have done enough today. I've got this."

Debbie set her dishes in the sink and then moved over and hugged Merry tight. "Love you, sweetie. Call me if you need me."

Merry nodded and went over to embrace Derek. Though he hugged her back, she could feel the tension in his muscles. "Love you, bro."

Derek pulled back and stared into his baby sister's face. "Love you too, Sis. Behave yourself."

Merry forced a smiled. "Always. Same goes for you two."

She watched them walk out to the moving van. In seconds, they were gone, a cloud of dust following right behind them. Satisfied they were out of sight, Merry made a beeline for the kitchen. She pulled out the dog food from the back of the cabinet, along with Percy's bowl. After filling his dish, Merry headed outside toward the barn, glad this was the last time she'd have to lock Percy up alone.

17

7:00 P.M. SATURDAY NIGHT

Derek pulled up behind Debbie's car and parked. "Well, here we are."

"Thanks for giving me a lift, Derek. I don't know about you, but it seems really strange to be sitting in front of this place knowing Merry doesn't live here anymore. I've had a lot of great times in there over the years."

Derek nodded while he stared out the windshield to the front door. "Yep, so did I. Of course, there were a lot of bad times as well. Can't blame her for wanting to leave."

Wiping a straggler tear from her cheek, Debbie cleared her throat. Derek felt the shift in the air.

"She has us to help her pick up the pieces. Carry the load when it becomes too heavy. No one in this world is tougher than my bestie. You are such a rock for her. She's lucky to have you as her brother."

"Thanks. I'm not sure I agree with the second part one-hundred percent, but the first? Absolutely."

Debbie reached down and grabbed her purse from the floorboard. She scrounged for her keys and said, "May I ask you something?"

Keeping the groan of irritation inside, Derek answered, "Of course. What's on your mind, Deb?"

Producing her best smile and smoldering stare, Debbie turned her face toward Derek's. "What did Mitchell say about me that sent Merry into such a tizzy?"

"That certainly wasn't the question I expected," Derek said, laughing.

Scooting closer, Debbie whispered, "Were you expecting something more along the lines of why haven't you kissed me yet?"

Unable to control himself, Derek felt the bulge press against the seam of his jeans. In all the years he'd known Debbie, this was the first time they'd ever been alone together for any extended period of time. She was beautiful and sexy as hell, and being this close to her, feeling the sexual heat roll off her in waves, was hard to resist. He was surprised at the throaty rumble in his voice when he answered, "Which question do you want me to answer?"

"Both."

She was so close Derek felt her warm breath graze his lips. "Mitch thinks you're hot and wished you didn't have eyes only for me. Because if you didn't, he wanted to take you home and ravage you. Doesn't understand why I haven't yet."

Debbie followed Derek's gaze to her chest and grinned seductively. Sensing he was close to caving in, she licked her lips and whispered, "Neither do I."

Hand controlled by his libido, Derek reached out and cupped a handful of her heavy breast. When she moaned, his dick turned to marble. He let his lips hover just above the skin on her neck, enjoying the way Debbie's flesh quivered.

"My place or yours?"

Debbie pulled away from Derek's embrace. "Mine's closer. Follow me."

In a flash, she was out of the van and in her car. With her intoxicating sensuality no longer at close proximity, he tried to clear his head. Think rationally. His hard cock had other ideas. It won the battle between mind and body. Derek started up the truck and followed Debbie home.

Derek knew he was dancing on thin ice. Though he'd always been attracted to Debbie, he steered clear for a variety of reasons, including what he'd told Merry. However, the long-standing friendship between his sister and Debbie was only a minor reason Derek had never let his other brain take over and give in to temptation. That was also the major reason he'd never married or remained in a committed relationship for any extended period of time:

He simply did not trust women.

Period.

Hadn't since the awful night his mom crashed her car.

The memory of seeing her mangled body crumpled in a heap inside the destroyed vehicle made him shudder. He could still smell the gas leaking from the tank. The sound of sirens in the distance and the muffled screams of agony from the driver's seat were just as clear in his mind as the night he heard them. Ethel Mae Clarke's last words sent chills up his spine.

"Forgive me, son."

The events of that night so long ago ranked as number two on the biggest mistakes of his life. The after effects of number one on the list crept out from the shadows. Derek sensed time was short before the lie stepped into broad daylight, destroying everything.

So, before sins of the past demolished his future, Derek decided to let his shields down and find comfort—no, escape—inside the arms of Debbie Rutherford.

* * *

Tad Tompkins snorted another line of coke from the coffee table. He needed the bump to clear his head after watching the local news. Ever since last week, when the news broke about Peppy, he'd been a nervous wreck. Paranoia set in after he heard about Mookie. He'd lost his two street dealers and was now forced to sell the entire shipment from Memphis on his own.

147

There was simply no way he would consider bringing others into the fold. Too risky. Even if he did get lucky and find replacements who weren't affiliated with any gangs—which was a deal breaker in his book—Tad was too nervous to involve more outsiders. Whether it was the coke talking or simply inborn instincts, Tad knew when to listen to his gut.

And his gut told him to remain a loner—at least for a while.

But that wasn't the only thing bothering him.

Almost a week had passed and he hadn't heard one peep from his partner, which was completely out of the norm.

At first, Tad chalked it up to him being busy with the investigation into Mookie's death, which was now being referred to on the news as a homicide. The second he heard the report, Tad went into disaster preparedness mode. He destroyed the burner phone he used to connect with his cohorts, thinking any minute the cops would bust his door down after viewing De'Shawn's cell phone.

He removed all but one of the heroin bricks the next night under the cover of darkness, making so many trips to the underground tornado shelter in his neighbor's yard, he'd lost count. The departure of the old bat was a blind stroke of luck. His neighbor decided to move into an assisted living center and put her house on the market last month. That was the only positive during the previous week.

For the next five days, Tad waited on pins and needles, jumping every time the phone rang or a vehicle drove by. He paced a hole in the living room rug while he mulled over whether to hit the clubs and at least try to make some money back. With no idea how the investigation was going, his mind conjured all sorts of ugly scenarios.

His biggest fear was whether other cops knew about him and were simply waiting to pounce.

He knew the video he sent to Mookie had been watched, so who viewed it?

But the one disturbing thought pushing him closer to a mental breakdown was *Am I next*?

Desperate for cash and unable to shake away the sensation something was really wrong, he caved and went clubbing on

Thursday. Fortunately, things hadn't changed much in the last five years. He ran into quite a few of the fools he used to party with and made a nice profit.

But hitting the club scene was tiring, dangerous, and beyond risky. Word would spread about "that guy" who sold drugs, eventually tickling the ears of the security guards or club owners.

Brain in overdrive and heart pounding, Tad stood and went to the bathroom. His motto had always been to live for the moment, so he wouldn't waste another stuck inside his house cowering like some whiny bitch.

While the hot water pounded his back, Tad made up his mind. He'd give the guy one more day. If he hadn't heard from him by early Monday morning, he would call in the big guns. Remind them of exactly what was at stake, and how easily lives could be destroyed in seconds.

Inside the steamy shower, Tad muttered, "If Theodore Paul Tompkins goes down, I damned well won't go alone."

* * *

Mitch polished off another beer and belched. He waited for his eyes to focus while peering at the small screen of his cell. Surprised the time was after ten p.m., he stood and went inside to piss and grab another brew. He stumbled a bit while he walked up the steps from the porch to the back door and wondered exactly how many beers he'd already downed.

When he reached the fridge and found the empty twelve-pack, he had his answer.

Too drunk to drive to get more beer, yet not trashed enough to pass out, Mitch retrieved the bottle of whiskey from the back of the cabinet. The hooch had been sitting on the shelf for years, one of the last remaining items left behind after Serena divorced him. Though he knew he'd regret the decision in the morning, he ignored the small voice warning him inside his head. He didn't even bother with a glass. Instead, he simply unscrewed the cap and took a hefty swig.

Once back out on the porch, he lit a smoke. Twenty years

ago, he told everyone he'd quit, which was true most of the time. When under tremendous stress, alone, and drunk, Mitch smoked like his grandfather used to—one right after another.

He glanced at the ashtray next to him and laughed at the overflowing mound of butts. In less than three hours, he'd already huffed his way through an entire pack. He tried to force his tight muscles to relax. Taking another drag, he stiffened when the scent of musk and cinnamon hit him.

"Damn you. Even in a haze of whiskey I can still smell you. Oh, wait! Maybe I haven't drunk enough." Mitch took another deep pull from the bottle. "Nope, that's not it either. You still stink. Really should consider wearing cologne that isn't so obnoxious."

The screen door and floorboards creaked when John Hudson walked across the porch. He stopped and leaned against the railing, arms crossed in a pose meant to be menacing. The lone bulb from the ancient ceiling fan cast an odd shadow across John's face, making him look like a marionette.

"You're a real jokester, Sinclair. Ever thought of trying your hand at standup? If not, you should, you know, since your days with the department are numbered."

Mitch took another drag and blew the smoke out in John's direction. "Nope. I prefer all my performances to be horizontal, not vertical. Unless, of course, the gal likes it standing up. Not many do, although Michelle did. Actually, she liked it every way." Even from across the room and in the dim light, Mitch could see his comment about John's ex struck a nerve. He graced the prick with a wicked grin.

"Was that supposed to be a dig? If so, you really need to lay off the sauce before you start trying to inflict verbal damage. You're a legend, but only in your little mind."

"And Michelle's."

"That whore spread her legs for anything with a woody. No skin off my back what she thinks or who she fucked."

Mitch snorted. "I'm too drunk to remember it verbatim, but the quote by some famous writer about protesting too much comes to mind."

"Though I do enjoy this mental jousting, discussing your sexual conquests, or lack thereof, is not why I'm here."

"Really? And here I thought you stopped by for some pointers on pleasing the ladies. Rumor has it you have a new toy who is quite younger than you. I'm sure you need all the help you can get."

Ignoring the jab, John remarked, "Report's finished and turned in. Not only was De'Shawn's death a homicide, but it's definitely tied to Ramirez."

"Well there's a newsflash I didn't see coming. Wow...you're good, Hudson. Give yourself a pat on the back."

"Thanks for the vote of confidence, Sinclair." John crossed the porch, snatching up a smoke from the open pack on the table. "I'm well aware that wasn't going to be a shock to you, and it isn't the reason I'm here. That I'm also sure is no surprise to you."

Mitch tried to keep his voice neutral and not let his frustration out. Considering how much he'd already drank, neutrality was next to impossible. "No shit, Sherlock. I'm acutely aware of why you decided to invade my house with your stench. You do enjoy your petty torments, don't you? Let me guess. You also enjoyed dismembering small animals as a child too?"

John flicked the lighter and touched the flame to the smoke. He exhaled a large plume into the humid night air, watching the tendrils swirl above him. "Only a matter of time before we nail the killer. When that happens, you know the press coverage will be brutal. Rogue cop offs not one but two poor souls trying to survive the poverty-ridden world they are stuck in. Ones who risked their lives and livelihood by giving information about bigger dealers to the police, only to have it backfire. Oh, I can just imagine what those notoriety-seeking bastards who call themselves civil rights activists will say. They'll probably hold a press conference out in front of the PD. Captain will love that."

Mitch couldn't control his seething fury. Though slower than normal, he was still faster than Hudson. Before the bastard had time to blink, Mitch had his hand around his throat and slammed Hudson up against the wall. "One more word and there'll be another homicide to investigate. If they ever find your body."

To Mitch's surprise, Hudson showed no fear. A twinkle of humor sparkled behind his ugly, dog shit brown eyes. Mitch gave a final squeeze and then let go.

John readjusted his wrinkled tie and grinned. He walked to the screen door, pausing before he exited. "Enjoy the rest of your evening, Sinclair. I'm sure I'll be seeing you again real soon."

"Not before I fuck your new girlfriend."

"That may be true, but as usual, you'll just be getting sloppy seconds." John stepped off the porch and disappeared into the darkness.

Mitch watched him until the undercover car turned left onto the main road and then threw the bottle against the side of the house. "Son-of-a-bitch! This isn't happening!"

Plopping down in the chair, he grabbed another cigarette. The nicotine didn't do much to calm his nerves. He jumped when his cell phone rang. Glancing down, he winced when he noticed the call was blocked, which meant it was probably one of his informants.

He was too fucked up to answer so he let it ring. A few seconds later, the phone beeped, notifying him the caller left a voicemail. Clicking the button, he put the phone to his ear and listened. By the time the message finished playing, he was shaking.

And wishing he still had the whiskey to numb the growing sense of panic burning inside his mind.

In the dark confines of the screened-in porch, Mitch mumbled, "This day sucked!"

18

"I'll have dinner hot and ready and the beer iced down by seven Friday night. Looking forward to seeing you again, Derek."

"Great. See you then."

Derek hung up before Debbie had a chance to say anything else. A twinge of guilt poked inside his stomach. After their night together on Saturday, the sex hot and sensual, he knew it had been a huge mistake bedding Debbie. He saw *the look* while she stared up at him in bed. The change in her voice would be obvious to a deaf person. Debbie Rutherford had fallen head-over-heels for him.

Too bad for her. When this is all over, she's going to hate me.

Derek stared out the window into the backyard. Memories of trying to teach Merry how to swim made his heart clench with sadness. Shifting his gaze back to the kitchen, Derek stared at the liquor cabinet where his father kept bourbon. When his mother was alive, it housed flour, sugar, and various cooking

153

essentials. After she passed, it was stocked full of whiskey and frequented at least three times a week by his heartbroken father.

For the next thirty years, until liver cancer sucked the life from his father.

Other than an occasional beer, Derek rarely drank. Tonight was different. He rose and went to the cabinet, extracting the dusty bottle of Jack and a shot glass. He poured a double and winced at the burning in his throat from the amber liquid. He repeated the motion three times before he sat back down at the kitchen table. What he'd hoped was the image on the computer screen in front of him would be different than before.

It wasn't.

The undeniable proof was right in front of him.

Two hours before, when he'd logged in to run the VIN number on Joshua's motorcycle, he'd told himself he was crazy. Merry said she'd sold it months ago, right around the same time she sold Harold's Jeep. Did his best to convince himself the nagging burn in his stomach was wrong. That a plausible explanation for the bag of dog food he'd found at Merry's was simply a leftover from the previous owner. Told his brain to believe Merry hadn't lied to him about how she sustained her injuries.

He downed another shot. More than anything in the world, Derek wanted to pretend he didn't know. Pretend his gut instincts weren't screaming inside him.

The cop wouldn't let the brother win.

All the circumstantial evidence converged together and formed the identity of Peppy and Mookie's killer.

His baby sister.

Unable to stand looking at the report that still listed Joshua Robert Clarke as owner of the Honda, Derek stared out into the backyard. The pool water shimmered under the silver rays of the bright moon, immediately bringing memories of the day Merry almost drowned. His father's admonition to always love and protect her made tears well up in his throat.

How am I supposed to protect her from herself?

He tried to push the tears away with another drink, but all it ended up doing was making him choke. In a fit of rage, he threw the glass across the kitchen, tears racing down his face at what he was about to do.

Brain spinning from the booze, it took him another ten minutes to force his hand to pick up the phone and scroll through his contacts until he located the number.

The familiar, gruff voice answered. "Better be important, Clarke."

Derek cleared his throat, forcing the tears back. "This is the most important conversation you and I will ever have, Captain."

19

7:00 P.M. THURSDAY NIGHT

"Well, what do you think?"

Merry twirled in a circle while Percy stared at her from his perch on the bathroom floor. His thick tail thumped against the old tile. He let out a garbled whine, his head tilting left and right as though confused by the short blonde wig on her head.

"I'm going to take your response to mean my outfit passes your inspection. Okay, so like I mentioned earlier, you can't come with me tonight. Riding shotgun while I'm stalking is one thing but quite another to be there when I kill. You might think less of me when you see what I'm capable of. You stay and guard the house, okay? I'll be back home soon I promise."

Exiting the bathroom, Merry grabbed her pack off the bed. She laughed after noticing all the dog hair on the comforter. Percy slept right next to her every night, occasionally giving her forehead a swipe with his wet tongue.

"I'm going to have to change from a white to a black comforter if you're going to continue to saw logs next to me all night. I don't even want to imagine how bad it would look if you had longer fur."

Percy's long nails clicked on the hardwood while he followed behind her. When she picked up her keys from the kitchen counter, Percy veered right and went to the front door. "You stay and relax, buddy. I think I heard a mouse in the kitchen earlier. Maybe you should entertain yourself searching for the little flea-carrier."

Percy tried to nudge his way out the front door, but Merry held out her hand. "Stay. I won't be long. I'm getting pretty good at dispatching people."

Tossing her bag into the passenger seat, Merry fired up the engine. Driving down the long drive, she let a wide grin appear. Her muscles tightened from the excitement of the hunt.

While she drove toward the city, she thought about the marathon conversation with Debbie on Sunday night. The girl was drunk off happiness. Thankfully, she spared Merry the intimate details of a night of debauchery with Derek but not the emotions associated with it.

At the time, Merry had been beyond thrilled the two of them finally connected. The excitement dimmed after talking to Derek on Monday night. Though he did acknowledge he'd spent the night with Debbie, he kept changing the subject. Merry sensed he didn't wish to discuss the matter.

He'd seemed off, edgy, and distant. Derek had talked about trivial, mundane things like he was having a conversation with a stranger standing in line at the grocery store, rather than his sister. She'd dismissed her worries, thinking he was too embarrassed to talk about something that less than two weeks ago, he swore would never happen.

Unwilling to broach the subject about Peppy or Mookie, Merry kept the TV in the living room on constantly. Since she no longer used her computer for fears her steps could be retraced, she switched back and forth between all three local news stations. Tonight's earlier broadcast was what she'd been waiting for—updates about the death of De'Shawn. Sure enough, it had been ruled a homicide.

Pulling onto the freeway, Merry reminded herself it didn't

matter. Forensics and good old police work figured out Mookie had been murdered, but they would never solve the case.

All those years of sitting in on trials certainly paid off. Taught me what not to do when committing a crime.

***

Less than forty-five minutes later, Merry arrived at her destination. She parked her car on the back side of the parking lot and cut the engine. No other cars were in sight, which wasn't much of a shock. At one time, Alsop Park had been full of parents watching their kids play on the swings or monkey bars, and the three baseball diamonds were full of adults who tried to relive their youth by playing softball.

But that had been years ago. Now the original colors of the playground equipment were faded or completely covered in orange rust. Weeds grew in the numerous cracks of the uncared for parking lot, and the baseball fields sported grass and weeds over two feet high.

The place was nothing but a blip in the memory of the residents of Little Rock, replaced by bigger, newer, and updated sporting complexes dotted the upscale communities on the other side of town. Of course, the real reason behind the demise of the once tranquil park was drugs.

Since the complex was off the beaten path and well hidden by groves of trees, all sorts of illicit activities migrated there. Before long, the place became a haven for drug dealers. After "white flight" happened and people began to move out west and into smaller bergs like Benton and Bryant, dealers concentrated their efforts near the clubs in downtown.

The old park was the perfect place to stash her car and make the two mile run to Tad's. She had spent two hours earlier studying her exact route and knew she would be flanking the backside of Tad's neighborhood.

While rummaging through the pack one final time, a twinge of worry rumbled in her stomach when she felt the knife. It bothered her earlier when she couldn't find her father's hunting knife, though she looked everywhere. Figuring it was simply misplaced during the move Merry stopped at a sporting goods store the day before and purchased a new one. She made a mental note to scour the house for the knife after taking out Tad.

Gear secured in her pack, Merry took off at a brisk pace. The last streaks of red and orange from the setting sun poked through the canopy of pine trees. She veered off into the woods. Knowing she only had about ten minutes of light left, Merry pushed her muscles to their limit.

By the time she neared the fence surrounding the backyards of Tad's neighbors, Merry was covered in sweat. The sun was gone, and the only light was from a few, sporadic porch lights from some of the homes. The one home she had her eye on, the empty house right next door to Tad's, was black, as was Tad's.

Perfect! Props to you oh gods of justice.

Merry bent over and yanked her running shoes off and then cinched up the boots. Gloves and vest in place, she secured the bag on her shoulders and hopped the fence for the second time in so many days. The dry run she'd made last night still hadn't been detected because Tad hadn't replaced the bulb she'd shot out with a slingshot. She wouldn't know if he'd discovered the thick coat of Vaseline slathered over the lens of both the front and backyard cameras until she was closer.

Though Tad's backyard was barren, the house next to him was full of a variety of shrubs and crepe myrtles, a good majority of them strategically interspersed along the invisible property line. Crouching, Merry kept her body close to the foliage until she was even with Tad's back porch. She scanned the area, holding her breath, watching and listening for any sounds of life near her position. Seeing and hearing nothing, she bolted from the trees and in seconds was on Tad's back porch.

The sticky goo on the lens was still there.

Wasting no time, Merry ran to the front of the house. She pulled short at the corner and peeked around. Tad's vehicle wasn't in the driveway, and no lights were on inside. Picking her steps carefully, she made her way to the front stoop and smiled.

The front camera was still covered, too.

After one more scan of the area, she cut across the driveway and over to the large gardenia bush next to the garage. She took the bag off, set it against the wall, and then situated herself next to it. All that was left to do now was wait...

And mentally go over every single detail she planned on doing to Tad Tompkins.

***

Other than the occasional bark from a dog in the distance, Chester Street had been quiet for two hours. A few times, she'd pulled out the binoculars from her bag and used them to scan the neighborhood just to have something to do. A house across the street and three houses down had the curtains open so Merry could see the TV. The last time she looked, the 10 o'clock news was on. When the owner turned off the set and the house went dark, Merry assumed it was after 10:30.

Stifling a yawn, Merry stretched. If the last four times she'd followed Tad were indicators, he wouldn't be home for another two or three hours. She was glad this mission was next to a fragrant flower bush rather than a reeking dumpster.

She saw the lights before she heard the vehicle. The rush of adrenaline made her skin prickle as the SUV neared and passed under the lone streetlight.

Tad.

Game time!

Stuffing the binoculars inside the pack, Merry extracted the long hunting knife from the side pocket. After securing the bag on her back, she rose slowly, keeping her back pressed against the wall. The sound of the garage door opening made her heart skip two beats while she watched the SUV pull into the drive.

The second the front grill disappeared inside the garage, Merry burst from her spot. In three steps she was at the back bumper, using the Tahoe for a shield. When it stopped, the big metal door closed and Merry held her breath, waiting for the sounds of Tad exiting the vehicle. The wait wasn't long.

She heard the driver's door open and the faint ding of an indicator of some sorts.

Tad's laughter bounced off the walls of the small place, making it sound like he was right next to Merry. "Duh, Tad. Got to unhook the seatbelt before you can get out."

The bastard erupted into a pile of giggles. Merry heard the jangle of his keys when they hit the ground. From his slurred speech, there was no doubt he was drunk and/or high.

Rather than confront him in the small space, Merry decided to remain still and let the fool extricate himself from the seat and head inside and then strike from behind. She listened to Tad fumble around, mumbling and cursing under his breath with the effort. Finally, the thud of his shoes when they hit the concrete was next, followed by footsteps to the door leading inside.

The duct tape on the bottom of Merry's boots suppressed the noise of her own footfalls. The second Tad's hand reached the doorknob, she stopped and steadied herself. When Tad pushed the door open and turned the lights on, Merry leaned back and executed a perfect side kick directly into his kidney.

Tad let out a weird grunt. His body flew forward nearly six feet, landing hard on the floor. Wasting no time, Merry yanked the bag from her back and opened it, retrieving two strands of nylon. Tad moaned and groaned but didn't move much except his arms and upper torso while he tried to roll over. Crouching next to his feet, she bound them in seconds.

"Enough whining you big baby. Stop acting like you've been shot or stabbed. Now, be a good boy and stretch your arms out over your head."

"Hey, baby," Tad responded while he struggled to roll over. "You want to play rough. I get that and I am so down with it. I've heard about chicks like you—ones who enjoy rape fantasies. You know, I always thought it was the other way around, but hey, I'm willing to play victim for a while. My only caveat is I want to switch roles later so I can play rough, too. You could have given me a heads up at the club though so I would've been better prepared for that wicked kick. So, do I need to struggle and scream for help, or just hold still and let you have your way..."

Tad's words dried up in his throat when he succeeded in

turning onto his back. The second he saw Merry, his grin disappeared, along with his hard-on.

"The latter is what I have in mind. Here," Merry instructed, tossing the rope to Tad. "Tie yourself up and let's head to the living room to chat. If you want to make it through this evening with all your body parts still attached, do as I say. Understand?"

To Merry's surprise, Tad burst out laughing, making the blood from his nose drip faster.

"You know, I hate being right sometimes! I knew I was next. I just had no idea it was you! Figures. Oh yes, let's have us a chat. There's no need for all this violence. Trust me, I'm going to enjoy our little talk. More than you know. Maybe after I share some of my deep, dark secrets with you, you'll have a change of heart about killing me."

Sensing his shift in attitude, Merry stiffened. She gripped the handle of the blade with more force.

Without any more prompting, Tad wound the rope around his wrists, using his mouth to tighten the knot. It took him a few tries but finally he stood and hopped his way down the hall toward the living room. Once he made it to the couch, he stopped.

"May I sit, or did you want to string me up first?"

"Toss me your phone then sit."

Tad turned sideways, exposing his back. "Right pocket."

Merry chuckled. She pulled the Glock from her back waistband. She pointed at center mass on Tad's chest. "Wow, you are really full of yourself, aren't you? Let's get a few things straight, Tad. I'm running this show, not you. I came here to get some information; however, I have no doubts I could obtain it from your phone and that laptop over there. My last two visits to drug dealers didn't end well for them because they didn't play by the rules. Now, take that phone out of your pocket nice and easy and set it on the table, or I'll remove it with a bullet."

"No, you won't."

For a second, Merry wondered if the sickness in her head had finally taken control. There was simply no way the voice from behind her, along with the familiar click of a hammer engaging, was real. Confirmation she was awake was given by

Tad's triumphant smile. His gaze shifted to the person behind her before he sat down and began to untie the rope around his ankles.

Part of her wanted to cry.

Another part deep inside her died.

The remaining bit of energy allowed Merry to remain upright. A thousand thoughts raced through her mind, speeding by so fast they made her dizzy.

The answer to her question about dirty cop or judge had just been answered, and the knowledge destroyed what was left of her small world.

"Drop the gun and knife, Merry."

With tears streaming down her face, Merry's voice was low yet defiant. "You'll have to kill me first, Derek."

"No, I won't."

The words were followed by a blow to the back of her head. For a split second, she felt the burning pain as stars danced in front of her eyes before collapsing onto the floor.

20

"Where were you five minutes ago? You know, before our dear Sis went all karate queen on my ass?"

"Shut up, Tad. I can't think straight with you blabbering."

"What's there to contemplate? I mean, you're here, and she's out cold just like we planned. Jesus, don't tell me you're getting all sentimental? I told you earlier, if you didn't have the balls to do this, I would. Just give me your gun..."

"I said shut up!" Derek roared, facing Tad. "And don't you ever refer to her as Sis again. Ever. She's my sister, not yours. You must be slipping. Recall our previous discussion about not killing her here? Get your wits back in order. Here, snort some more coke to wake yourself up."

Tad held his hands up in mock surrender after catching the baggie full of drugs Derek tossed. "Okay, okay, hoss. Chill. I get why you don't enjoy that little familial technicality. Didn't mean to offend or step on your toes. I'm only trying to help keep us both out of prison. A cop and a judge's son wouldn't last a year."

Ignoring the dig, Derek pointed to the couch. "You can help by tossing me the rope over here. Then, bring the chair."

Tad set the drugs on the coffee table and then threw the nylon pieces across the living room. Derek caught them and bent down and bound Merry's arms and legs. He slid his arms underneath her limp torso and hefted it onto the computer chair after Tad set it next to him. Once she was situated, he focused his attention back to Tad.

"Give me your phone."

Tad furrowed his brow. "What? Why?"

"We talked about this already, you idiot. Nothing electronic to track you while you dump her body, remember? And before you leave, we'll need to disable the GPS in your Tahoe. Think, Tad. Use what little brain cells you have left or we'll end up in prison."

Tad slapped his forehead and then extracted his cell and handed it to Derek. "Right! Sorry. Hey, cut me some slack, will you? This is my first murder. I'm not a seasoned, hardcore pro like you. Plus, I'm still a bit shell-shocked after the last twenty-four hours. I mean, talk about some freaky shit! Never pictured her as the violent type, much less a killer. Bet you didn't, either. What a fucked-up family, huh? To think, our partnership started so you could protect her little feelings, and the whole time, she was hunting us."

Derek's anger rose fast. He forced his arms to remain at his side. Instead of commenting on Tad's baited statement, he changed the subject. "You've got a long journey ahead of you tonight. My contact will meet you in Memphis at three a.m., not a minute later. I already put the instructions in the front seat of your vehicle."

Tad smiled. "So that's why you were late saving me, huh? Figures. Well, guess I better wake myself up then. I hate driving at night. So, I just meet the dude? Do I kill her before or after? Give me some guidance here."

Derek watched Tad move to the couch and dump out a pile of white powder on the table. "That's entirely up to you. My only rule is to make it quick and painless. Personally, I would wait until the meeting. They've already got a place off the grid to bury her, so no sense in ruining your vehicle."

Tad paused and stared at Derek before his first snort. "You're one cold-hearted bastard, I'll give you that. Knew it the first time we met. Gotta say, I was terrified you would shoot me rather than become my partner-in-crime."

Derek let a sly grin tug at his lips. "Speaking of partner-in-crime, how are sales? Are we close to needing another shipment?"

"So-so. Club scene isn't nearly as profitable like street sales. You have Si—I mean, Merry—to thank for that. On the lookout for some new dealers to help us along, but none have cropped up yet. Won't need another batch for at least a month."

"Really? Seems odd, since I didn't find any here earlier, and I looked. Everywhere. You wouldn't be so stupid as to hold out on me, right?"

Tad took a hefty snort and wiped his nose. "Hell no. Bricks are all stashed in the storm shelter next door. No worries—the house is empty, so no one has a clue. I did it as a safety precaution. You're saying you snooped around my place while I was gone? Not cool, hoss. Not cool."

Tad lowered his head and snorted another thick line. Derek used the opportunity to snatch Tad's cell from the table. After extracting his own, he sent a quick text. He glanced at Merry, worried she would come to any second. Tad worked on his third bump when a stream of blood oozed from his nose.

"Shit! I feel...this is...wrong. What did you...?"

Derek watched Tad collapse back into the couch. Blood leaked from Tad's nose and ears, covering his shirt in crimson. Derek pulled his gun and reached over to grab a cushion. "Gave you a little going away present—a speedball. Got to set the stage so there will be no doubts when the crime scene is processed. You were right to be terrified of me, Tad. My biggest regret is not doing this before."

"No, please!"

Derek ignored Tad's mumbled plea. Before the bastard had a chance to move or say another word Derek lunged. The pillow and gun inches from Tad's bloodied face, he fired. The cushion muffled the sound and helped keep the blood spatter off Derek.

"You were right—this has all been about protecting my sister."

Derek stiffened when he heard Merry moan. Holstering his weapon, he tossed the pillow to the floor while studying Tad's destroyed face. There was no doubt the rat bastard was dead, so Derek walked over to sit down across from his sister. Nervous energy thrummed through his body, expelled through his legs. He was helpless to stop them from bouncing while he waited for his sweet baby sister to awaken.

❊ ❊ ❊

Merry's head pounded, the majority of the pain centered in the back. Dazed, unsure if awake or dreaming, she struggled to grasp the sounds tickling her ears. She could tell two men were talking but couldn't make out the words. Panic welled-up inside her when she tried to move and discovered her hands were bound.

Think! The last thing I remember I was at Tad's. We were in the living room...a voice behind me...oh, God, no. Please, please let this be a nightmare. Let me wake up next to Percy. Please?

Merry's eyes flew open at the precise moment full clarity of what previously happened hit. Blinking twice to focus, her heart rate spiked when her gaze settled on Tad's dead body.

And Derek sitting less than ten feet away.

Confusion made her stomach roll. "Derek?"

"Sorry about your head, Sis. I tried not to break the skin, only hit hard enough to immobilize you for a few minutes. Had things to take care of before you woke up."

Merry glanced at the mess on the couch and then down at the bloody cushion on the floor. When she noticed the pile of powder on the table, she stiffened. "You rang my bell hard enough you'll need to explain what the fuck is going on with small words, brother."

Derek took in a deep breath and whispered. "Finding the right words to say is harder than I thought."

Merry could see the utter anguish etched across Derek's face. His legs were bouncing—an annoying habit since childhood when stressed—and droplets of sweat beaded across his brow. She scrambled the pieces of the puzzle she knew in her head and tried to form a clear picture. When the strange shapes melded together, she felt her stomach drop.

"When did you realize it was me?"

Derek let a feeble grin appear. "The burn in my gut started when Mookie called me right after you paid him a visit. Pushed the feelings aside because he said the woman had black hair and a tattoo. When I saw your bruises, the burn ignited and again, I ignored it. Wanted more than anything to believe your story. After I found the dog food at your new place, I ran the VIN on Joshua's bike. Once I confirmed you still owned it, I've been following you ever since."

Dumbstruck, Merry said, "You were Mookie's handler?"

Derek gave one quick nod for his answer, his eyes averted from Merry's intense stare.

A few seconds of silence passed between them while Merry digested the news. Thoughts were spinning so fast inside her mind she felt dizzy. "And here all this time I pegged Mitch for the dirty cop. Why, Derek? What in the world happened that pushed you into this world?"

"You."

Anger made Merry's voice louder. "Me? What the fuck kind of excuse is that, Derek?"

Derek pulled his gaze from the floor and found Merry's eyes. "Do you remember your first day of fishing and how you nearly drowned?"

"I don't see…"

Derek held up his hands. "Give me a chance to explain. I promise you'll understand everything when I'm done. Okay?"

Merry never said a word in response. Instead, she used the opportunity of Derek being distracted to work on freeing her hands.

"I didn't want you to go with us. I liked my alone time with Dad. Made a big stink about it and got my ass whooped. Dad made me swear to take care of you—to protect you from harm—no matter what. I took it to heart and have been ever since."

Though she tried to stop herself, Merry shot back. "What part about whacking me from behind and tying me up falls into the protective category?"

Derek rose and yelled, "Shut up and listen, Merry!"

Watching Derek pace back and forth made the hairs stand up on Merry's neck. Since he was armed and she was his captive, Merry decided to switch tactics. "Derek...calm down, please? My head is throbbing, and I'm scared. All of this makes no sense, and I'm trying to follow what you're saying, but it's difficult."

"I'm probably rambling, which isn't helping you. This whole mess is hard for me to articulate, believe me. I opened with that story because protecting you—even if it means from yourself—is what I've been doing your entire life, and what ended up pulling me into this ugly world."

Softening her tone, Merry asked, "So, you figured out I was the killer and decided to stop me, yet you killed Tad?"

Derek's face flushed with anger. "I have wanted to blow his fucking head off for years. That bastard is the reason we both are here."

"Come again?"

Derek let out a huff of air while running his fingers through his hair. "Tad...knew things he shouldn't have about our family. He used them to get me—and another—to comply with his requests. If we didn't, he threatened to expose certain things you never needed to know."

Stunned, Merry said, "That piece of shit knew things about our family? How? What things were so damned explosive you never wanted me to know, Derek? Stop being so cryptic and just spit it out!"

The minute the words left her mouth, Merry sensed the electrical shift in the room. Derek never answered with words, only with his eyes. She knew who stood in the doorway before he ever spoke.

"I'm afraid my son enjoyed holding us both hostage, dear. He forced us to play in his sick game. We did so to keep you from discovering the truth about me—and your mother."

Shocked into silence, Merry watched Judge Tompkins enter the room. His gaze never wavered from her own, big brown eyes full of tears. Bypassing his dead son, the judge stopped and knelt down, placing a warm hand on her calf.

His touch sent waves of anger throughout her body. "Get your hands off me, you liar! You two are out of your minds! Oh, better yet—maybe high on the shit you've been dealing? You must be if you think I'll believe you both turned dirty because you had an affair with my mother and didn't want me to find out. That is the most pathetic excuse I've ever heard in my life! Joshua came up with better lies when he was higher than a kite!"

Tears rolled faster down Judge Tompkins' wrinkled cheeks. Behind his eyes, Merry saw the deep sadness, the unspoken words. Memories of the past flooded back. Closing her eyes, Merry shook her head to make them disappear as tears of her own appeared.

21

1:00 A.M. FRIDAY MORNING

"We didn't mean for it to happen. Your father was my best friend. We went to the academy together—lived through some really close calls while on the streets. Your mother and I were friends—nothing more—for years. Things changed as time passed. I found myself looking forward to dinner at the house to enjoy her company, not your father's. We knew it was wrong and never verbalized our feelings or succumbed to temptation for a long time. Not until one night when your mother was alone and Derek was sick. Your dad was out of town..."

Forcing the bile back down, Merry whispered, "Enough. I get it. I'm the product of a one-night stand by two pieces of shit. Makes sense why you disappeared from our lives. Must say I'm surprised my dad—you know, the one who raised me knowing I was a bastard child—didn't kill you. What, were you two afraid that's what my reaction would be or something? That I'd go all crazy and kill the upstanding judge?"

"Of course not. We both knew how close you were to your

father. Didn't want to tarnish your memory of him...or of your mother."

Merry glared at the judge. "Bullshit. You didn't want your precious reputation to be tarnished. The high-and-mighty conservative judge wanted his skeletons to stay locked inside a dark closet. Don't even try to give me this song and dance of worrying about how I'd take the news. What's your excuse, Derek? Try something other than this whole protective-brother skit. I'm not falling for that. I'm sure it's more along the lines of needing some fast cash."

Derek and Judge Tompkins traded places. Merry watched Derek's expression turn ice-cold. Felt a heavy sense of dread and fear settle over hear heart.

"I found out you were only my half-sister the night Mom died. Dad and I both did. You were spending the night at Debbie's, and I was in my room, listening to them scream at each other about your recent doctor's visit. Since Dad had O+ blood, when he saw your blood type was B, he knew immediately he wasn't your father. Dad was drinking heavily and ended up passing out before either of them actually mentioned the name of her lover. Mom left and I followed, angry she'd betrayed Dad. At the time, I had no idea the mystery lover was Ron. When she pulled up at his house, I lost it. Called her a whore. Told her I hated her for what she'd done. Threatened to return to the house and get Dad's service revolver and come back to kill them both."

"Oh, my God," Merry whispered. "You caused her accident, didn't you?"

Tears welled-up inside Derek's eyes. "Yes. She tried to catch me, but my motorcycle was faster than her car. She rolled her car in a curve. I stood there, full of anger and hate, and watched her burn to death. I could have helped her, but I didn't. When Ron showed up, he tried but was too late. He knew what I'd done and never said a word. I left and went home, and things have been fucked up ever since."

"Jesus, this isn't happening."

Judge Tompkins finally looked at the remains of his son on the couch. "It's my fault Tad found all this out. One night, on the thirtieth anniversary of your mother's death, I had too much to drink. Tad found me in my study, slumped over pictures of your mother—and you—lamenting the past mistakes of my life. I opened up to my son, hoping to find some comfort, but instead, he turned on me. Within a week, he had Derek and me cornered. I've been paying for my past transgressions ever since. A sentence handed down by my own flesh and blood."

Derek nodded in agreement. "We were trapped, Merry. Tad knew Joshua was an addict. He threatened to sell Joshua tainted dope if I didn't cooperate with his scheme. That's why I beat up Peppy. When I found out Joshua was one of his regulars, I swore I'd kill him if he ever sold him dope he hadn't first tried before selling to Joshua."

"Wow...what a great uncle you are!" Merry snapped.

"We considered telling you, but you were going through so much with Joshua, we were afraid of how you'd take it. I feared you'd have a heart attack or stroke. I certainly never thought things would turn out the way they did. Not in a million years."

"Again, I call bullshit. Don't either of you dare try blaming me for bad choices. You know, you could have just let me go to my grave without knowing all this. Why tell me now?"

Derek rose and removed the Glock from the holster. "Because you decided to go on a killing spree. When we realized it was you—and that Tad was next in line—we agreed it was time to end it"

Merry couldn't take her gaze off the gun. "By killing me? That's the solution?"

"No, Sis. I've already killed two family members. I won't make it three."

"Two?"

"The night he died, Joshua saw the drug deal go down between me, Peppy, and Tad. Peppy played us. Told Josh ahead of time, and he showed up and recorded us. I chased him down the alley and took the phone. He refused to listen to me. Kept yelling about how he wouldn't let me get away with it—that he planned on telling you and my superiors—regardless of whether I destroyed his phone or not. I couldn't let that happen, so I held him down and forced him to snort enough to stop his heart."

The disconnect inside her mind happened the second Derek's words registered.

Merry wanted to scream, call Derek every foul word she'd ever heard. Wanted to lunge from the chair and use her head as a battering ram. Wanted to free her hands, find the gun, and silence his deceitful mouth.

How would she ever get past the pain? The betrayal? A lifetime of lies and deception, all culminating with Joshua's murder?

Brain on information overload, numbed by the words, Merry simply stared at her brother like she'd never seen him before. In truth, she hadn't, for the man standing in front of her was a monster—one who killed her only son. The spinning thoughts from before were gone, replaced by bone-crushing pain. The sensation enveloped her and began to constrict the air from her lungs.

The sound of the judge's voice was faint and distant. "That's why we devised this plan, dear. The time to atone for our mistakes is now, and our final act will ensure no one will ever discover what you've done. After all, you wouldn't have been driven to madness if not for our actions."

"That's right. I'm able to say my final act will fulfill the promise I made to Dad: I'm protecting you."

"Yes, darling daughter, we both are because we love you so much. Please, try to find it in your heart someday to forgive us."

Merry heard Derek chamber a round, but it didn't really register until another voice rumbled, "Drop the gun, Derek. I won't ask twice."

Before she could get her brain to comprehend it was Mitch's voice, Derek said, "I left you something in your mailbox you'll need to retrieve as soon as possible. You know, I get why you did all this, Merry. You wanted those responsible for Joshua's death to pay. Now, they finally will. Forgive me, Sis."

Inside her mind, Merry screamed, "*Go to hell, you bastard!*" Had she said it out loud, the words would have been drowned out by gunfire.

Two shots ended the lives of the Honorable Ronald Arthur Tompkins and Detective Derek Isaac Clarke. Blood seeped from the wound in the Judge's chest, the bullet from Derek's gun. Merry looked away and stared at the body of Derek. He was less than a foot from her, blood pouring from the gaping hole in his head, the bullet courtesy of Mitch's.

Mitch was by her side in a flash. He untied the rope and grabbed Merry by the shoulders, shaking her out of catatonia. "Leave. Now. Go home and clean up. Don't stop. Don't talk to anyone. Go!"

The look of concern and heartbreak behind Mitch's eyes was enough. Merry knew he meant every word, and somehow, he'd make sure to leave her name out of the events on Chester Street. Without saying a word or taking one last look at the carnage in the living room, she rose and exited the back door into the dark night.

❃ ❃ ❃

Merry pulled up in the driveway and shut the engine off. On autopilot, she got out of the car and stumbled up the walkway. After three attempts to unlock the door, she managed to make it inside and turn on the light. Percy jumped around like happy puppy while following her down the hall. She stopped by the kitchen and rummaged around the junk drawer until she found a pack of matches before heading out the back door.

My brother killed my son.

She walked across the yard to the burn barrel. Once stripped of all her clothes, she threw them into the drum and set them on fire. Under the cover of night, the only witnesses Percy and the stars above, Merry watched the flames devour her clothes.

My mother.

Satisfied nothing remained but a pile of ashes, she turned and went back inside.

While standing under the hot spray of the shower, the numbness previously engulfing her being started to dissipate. The emotional impact of the evening hit her—hard. Merry sank down into the tub at the same time great sobs erupted from her shattered heart.

My entire existence.

✳ ✳ ✳

Unable to sleep and tired of pacing while she waited for the rest of her world to explode, Merry had decided to finally read Joshua's journal before her mind completely shut down. For three hours she sat on the bed, Percy curled next to her, and choked back the tears while she read. The parts where Joshua let out his deepest fears and regrets made her cry again, but the parts near the end when he was sober made her swell with pride.

Journal entry – January 12th

Sober for five months! Nothing in this world compares to seeing the smile on Mom and Dad's face. Especially Mom. God, I've hurt them both so much—and knowing that makes me want to numb the shame and humiliation with drugs. What a vicious cycle! I won't give in—I won't. I need to learn to live with the ups and downs of life with a clear head. Hang on to the pain so it will remind me of what drugs did to me and my family.

On a lighter note...I had a chance today to help another addict. What a great experience! Peppy wants out of the life. Said I inspired him to get clean. Meeting him tonight to talk about treatment options and to find out what he wants to discuss in person. He seemed really scared on the phone earlier. Said what he had to tell me would hurt a lot of people. Must admit it feels really great knowing my successes have given someone else hope they can change as well. Even though I love working with my dad, maybe accounting isn't what I'm supposed to be doing. Maybe I should check into being a drug counselor? I'll make sure to talk to my sponsor tonight and ask him what he thinks. Oh, the look on Mom's face when I tell her I want to go to college! She'll be so happy. I hope one day she'll even be proud.

Clutching the journal to her chest, Merry whispered, "I am proud of you, baby. God, so very proud."

22

Percy heard the car before Merry did. He jumped off the bed and ran to the window, hackles raised and a snarl on his lips. Merry stood and tightened her robe, knowing who pulled up without even looking. She turned and opened the bedroom door and exited before Percy had a chance to follow, shutting the door behind her. Rather than going to the front door, she headed to the kitchen to pour another cup of coffee.

Car doors slammed.

Footsteps on the porch.

Three quick knocks on the door.

The fuse is lit. Time to drop the bomb.

The distance from the hallway to the kitchen to the door seemed miles away. With tentative steps, Merry made her way across the floor, her mind in a foggy haze. Somehow, her vocal chords seemed to take on a life of their own, and she was shocked when she heard herself say, "Who is it?"

"Merry? It's Mitchell Sinclair, your brother's partner?"

Mouth dry and heart pounding, Merry opened the door. Her voice sounded muffled when she said, "Mitch, what are you doing here?"

Three men stood on the porch: Captain Guss, Mitchell, and another Merry didn't recognize. The Captain and the other man exchanged glances. The stress of the situation hung in the air like an invisible blanket.

Captain Guss spoke first. "Mrs. Hall, we need to speak with you. There's...a situation involving your brother. May we come in?"

The words sent Merry's thoughts back to the morning her father came to pick her up at Debbie's.

Once they reached home, all the tears and hugs when he gathered her into his strong arms and broke the news about the accident.

The terror thrumming inside her little chest while watching her father cry while trying to grasp the meaning of the words.

Seeing Derek sitting on the opposite end of the couch, head buried in his hands.

Mom's funeral.
Joshua's funeral.
Harold's funeral.
Soon, Derek's.

The coffee cup she'd been holding shattered when it hit the floor. The room spun and sounds around her were distant and muffled. A male voice yelled. "I've got her!" It was followed by another. "Get her to the couch."

Then, dark silence.

❅ ❅ ❅

"I'm taking you to the hospital. You're really pale."

Merry removed the cold rag from her head and sat up. "No, you aren't. I'm fine." She glanced around the living room. "How long have I been out?"

"About ten minutes."

"When did you get here, and where'd they go?"

Debbie took the rag and handed Merry a glass of water. "Pulled up in time to see you pass smooth out. Mitch is outside trying to convince them to leave and let us break the news to you instead of two strangers. Should be easy to convince them. I'm sure you slamming into the ground the second you saw them on the porch was confirmation enough."

Red and white stars appeared for a second, replacing the image of Debbie's tear-stained face. Merry waited until they disappeared before she answered. "How did you hear?"

Tears formed behind Debbie's eyes. She blinked several times to force them back. "When the judge didn't show up for court today. I had just dialed his cell around nine when Renee from accounting burst in, sobbing like crazy. She was so distraught, she couldn't really talk. She simply turned on the TV. It's all over the news, although their names weren't mentioned. Of course, we all knew it was Judge Tompkins since he wasn't there. Tried calling you, but you didn't answer, so I came over instead. Since I don't see Derek here, I assume...?"

Merry watched her closest friend attempt to remain strong and not cry but knew it wouldn't last long. The tears from seconds ago were back, racing down Deb's flushed face. Unwilling to even speak her brother's name, much less talk about him, Merry simply nodded.

Debbie's clammy hand shook as she clasped Merry's. "I...don't even know what to say, sweetie, other than I'm here for you and love you. I'm so very sorry."

Mitch cleared his throat. "Sorry to interrupt. Just wanted you to know they left."

"Do they know...everything?" Merry asked.

Mitch walked over and leaned against the fireplace. "No."

Debbie's gaze bounced between Mitch and Merry. "What's going on?"

From the back bedroom came Percy's low whine.

"Is that a dog?" Debbie asked, incredulous.

Balance still off and head throbbing, Merry stood and pulled Debbie up with her. "Yes. His name's Percy. I...just recently acquired him. He was...a stray in the woods." Turning her gaze back to Mitch, Merry continued. "She deserves to know

181

the truth about Derek, Mitch. So do I. Come on, let's take Percy out for a walk, and I'll start with what I know first. You can fill in the rest."

Merry could see the distrust behind Mitch's eyes while he stared at Debbie. "You sure? I'm already walking a thin line just by talking about all this."

With one last squeeze, Merry let go of Deb's hand. "Yes, I'm positive. You know the news won't get all the facts straight. Now, you two stay here while I get Percy. Not sure how he's going to react to strangers."

"I'm so confused." Debbie threw her arms up in frustration.

"You won't be in a few minutes. Promise. That is, if you really want to know. If you'd prefer to remain in the dark—"

"If things get any darker, I'm going to do a face-plant. Whatever's on your mind, I'm here for you. Always have been, always will be."

❋❋❋

Other than the sounds of a few birds and insects, the back porch was silent. It had taken three full hours to explain to Debbie what had happened, and why. Merry left out her role as killer, determined not to burden Debbie with the knowledge. It wouldn't be fair to risk it, and besides, one person already knew, and that was enough.

To her credit, Debbie held her emotions in check for the most part, only truly breaking down when Merry got to the part about Joshua. By the time Merry finished, Debbie no longer could contain her tears. Neither could Merry. They clung to each other and wept for what once was, what could have been, and what would never be. Each of them cried for the sadness of so many lives destroyed over money, drugs, and misplaced loyalties.

For fifteen minutes, the three of them sat lost in their own thoughts while they watched ducks come and go from the pond. After a thorough sniffing earlier, Percy seemed to accept two new people in his life and ignored both Mitch and Debbie, preferring to stretch out over Merry's feet. While the silence gave each a chance to catch their mental breaths, especially Debbie, it was time to move on. She hoped Debbie had recovered from the shock because she needed to hear what Mitch had to say before she dropped the last bombshell.

"Tell me your story, Mitch."

Debbie and Merry waited while Mitch took a swig of beer. After a deep breath he focused his gaze on the pond. A dark shadow of sadness swept across his face.

"I didn't suspect anything until a few months after Joshua's death. Derek started acting odd, saying strange things in passing. Talked about retiring, which he had previously said he'd never do until he was too old to take someone down. Mentioned numerous times how he regretted not marrying, yet in the next breath, complained about how even being a family member wasn't a guarantee the person was someone you could love or trust. At first, I chalked it up to the strain of losing his nephew and his constant worrying about you. Then he started screwing up at work, coming in late, not completing reports. He'd be gone for half a day or more and wouldn't answer the phone. I called him out about it once, and he flew into a rage. I knew then something was wrong. Really wrong. I'm usually the one who loses it, not Derek."

"Why didn't you come and talk to me?" Merry asked.

Mitch let out a long sigh. "In retrospect, I should have. You were going through so much of your own issues I didn't want to pile on more. Like I said, at first I thought he was just struggling to work through the emotions of the situation. It wasn't until one of the guys we went to the academy with, Detective Russell Morrison, called me several weeks ago. He works narcotics in Memphis and witnessed Derek buying a load of heroin from one of the dealers on their squad's watch list."

"Oh, dear Jesus," Debbie whispered. "Figures. I've always loved a bad boy. Good Lord, I think I'm going to need another beer. No, several."

Merry reached over and gave a gentle pat on Debbie's trembling arm. "Me, too."

Mitch stood, pacing across the porch while smoking. "I didn't want to believe it. Called the guy a liar. Told him he was full of shit. Asked him to give me time to investigate on my own, and if he was right, I'd get Derek help. He agreed since it happens so much on the job. Cops get addicted to a substance—or the money, even sometimes both. It's not a surprise. The risk of abuse is another reason why most only work up to a max of two years in narcotics before rotating to another unit. Morrison gave me one month. So, I attached a tracking device on Derek's truck. The night De'Shawn Majors died, Derek went to Memphis. Detective Morrison called me and said he saw him there. I logged in to check out Derek's location and was shocked to see not only had he been to Memphis but was parked in front of Mookie's."

Things were still fuzzy inside Merry's head. It took her several seconds to soak up the words while she remembered the night at De'Shawn's. To no one in particular, she mumbled, "Those were the headlights I saw."

"What?" Debbie asked.

"I'll explain later. Mitch, how did you end up at Tad's?"

"Captain called me in first thing Thursday morning. Told me Derek called him late Wednesday night, drunk, and quit the force. Asked me to go check on him, which I did, but he wasn't home. I called and sent several texts, but he never answered. Not until he sent me a text late last night. It simply said 'coffee's hot, need some ice' and the address. It was our personal code for drug bust happening, weapons involved, and to arrive silently. I knew the second I read it things would be bad, but I was wrong. They were awful. Believe me I was shocked when I heard him confess. Really didn't think he'd actually pull the trigger and kill the judge, but he proved me wrong."

Debbie's eyes widened. "Did you...are you...the officer who shot Derek?"

"Yes," Mitch replied in a low whisper. He turned to face Merry. "I can't even begin to express how sorry I am for that. The memory will haunt me the rest of my life, yet it pales in comparison to what awful images haunt yours."

Locking gazes with Mitch, anger crept into Merry's voice. "Don't be. You were just doing your job, Mitch. Derek did this to himself. Ruined my life." Merry paused to regain her composure.

"I'm grateful the real monster responsible for Joshua's death is dead."

Debbie shook her head in disbelief while gulping down the remainder of her beer. "There are no words I can think of to capture how stunned I am. I mean, good God! We worked for what looks like to be one of the biggest crooks in the state! Never, in a million years, would I have ever suspected Judge Tompkins capable of this. Never. All this death—it's just too surreal. I've got to be at home having a nightmare. I can't even fathom how you must feel, sweetie. Must say, you're handling the news better than I am!"

"Well, there's a reason I seem sort of...off." Casting a quick glance over to Mitch, Merry swallowed hard and cleared her throat. In a low monotone, she explained to them both something she'd only discussed with one other person—Dr. Cash.

When she finished forty minutes later, all three of them were crying.

23

10:00 A.M. THURSDAY MORNING

Debbie helped Merry finish getting ready for the funeral. The bouts with dizziness and balance, coupled with the raging migraines, occupied up to fifty percent of Merry's days now. Though she hated admitting it, she needed assistance. Debbie had forced Merry to go see Dr. Cash on Monday, insisting she needed to hear the news from the doctor's mouth, not Merry's. He not only explained to Debbie what went wrong inside Merry's brain, but also warned the inoperable glioblastoma in her frontal lobe had expanded—fast. The original prognosis of two months—which Merry surpassed three months ago—was whittled down to one week.

Fifteen minutes of tears—again—followed after they made their way out to Debbie's car. In the parking lot of St. Vincent's Memorial, the two friends tried in vain to comfort one another at the news.

Debbie had been by her side—just like Percy—ever since.

Merry dropped a makeup brush and squatted down to get

it. Percy whined and nudged her head with his own. Debbie chuckled. "Guess it's true what they say about dogs."

Before Merry had a chance to reach out to steady herself, Debbie grabbed her hand and helped her up. "I've wondered the same thing. I mean, he took to me so quickly. Of course, he took to you right away and didn't rip Mitch's face off, so it could be he simply is a great judge of character."

"I'm glad he likes me." Debbie gave Percy's head a gentle pat. "With him around, I won't be so scared out here alone at night."

"Nope. He's a great companion. So, is it about time? I'm ready to get this atrocity over with. The thought of forcing myself to pretend I'm the heartbroken sister makes me nauseated. Galls me to no end to bury the bastard in our family's plot. At least I won't be faking it when I leave right after because of a headache. You did put in the obituary only a grave-side service, right?"

Debbie smiled. "Yes, sweetie. Got to say, I'm more concerned about the press. They're going to hound you. This mess has been the opening story on every channel since last Friday."

Unable to control her anger, Merry grumbled, "If they want to risk getting close to this mouth, let them. I'll certainly give them an earful not fit for TV or print."

"That you would my friend. Nobody can hold a candle to you when you're all fired up. What did that one guy in high school call you when you slashed his tires after you caught him with that cheerleader?"

A snide grin appeared on Merry's lips. "Maniacal Merry."

"Yes! That's it."

Shooing Debbie from the bathroom, Merry moved to the bed and sat on the edge. "Mitch said he'd make sure to keep them out, so we should be good. He's turned out to be quite a godsend throughout this whole thing. Feel sort of bad now considering how I felt about him before...and what I said to him that day in the living room."

Debbie helped slide Merry's shoes on. "Stop dwelling on

something you can't change. Besides, if you haven't noticed he's forgiven you, you're blind. He's been here every day!"

"Considering he was on paid leave while under investigation from the shooting, what else was he supposed to do?"

"He could have done a lot of things, none of which included being around you. Think about that. Enough about Mitch. Hey, at least we've been safe here. I mean, not one journalist has poked a nosey snout down your road."

"That was my hope when I created the trust and bought this place. Hopefully, they never will, and you and Percy can live here in peace."

"Damn, Merry! You promised me you wouldn't make me cry today! I...still can't believe you did this for me. I mean, you didn't know all the particulars, the way things would work out..."

Merry grabbed both of Debbie's hands, her gaze intense while she looked into the eyes of the kindest soul she'd ever encountered. "I can't change the way our lives worked out my friend, and I'm so sorry Derek hurt you. Regardless of all the other things that happened, it didn't matter at the time I made the decision. I knew I was dying, and my reason to buy this house was strictly based on you. I wanted your time left here to be tranquil and a daily reminder of better times. God knows the world is full of enough bad ones. I want you to enjoy the money and the house. There is enough cash to give you time to work full time on your art pieces so you can do your part to bring joy and beauty to an ugly world."

Debbie dabbed her eyes with a tissue. "Remember all the times I said you were strong and amazing? I was wrong. You are the freakin' Rock of Gibraltar. God, I can't believe throughout all the turmoil in your life, you thought about me. I...love you so much."

Merry pulled Debbie close and hugged her, inhaling their friendship like it was sweet cologne. Her last act of kindness wasn't even close to balancing the scales of other deeds, yet it felt marvelous.

Finished with her notes, Merry gathered them up along with two binders. She rose from the desk and made Percy stay in her room and then padded down the hallway toward the kitchen. She could hear Mitch rummaging around in the fridge.

"Hope I didn't wake you."

Merry motioned for Mitch to follow her out to the back porch. "You didn't. Been working on something I need to give you. Sleep is my enemy these days."

Once situated outside, Merry slid the binders across the table to Mitch.

"What's this?"

"Before I tell you, I need to get a few things off my chest. First and foremost, I owe you an apology."

"That tumor of yours really has messed with your thought patterns. You have that backward—I owe you..."

Merry held up her hand. "Stop and let me finish. I'm sorry for assuming you were the bad guy. In my quest for revenge, I'd already resigned myself to killing you, thinking you were next in line. Plus, I really never gave you much of a chance. Always assumed you were an ass."

Mitch chuckled. "According to everyone else, I am."

"That may be true in their world, but in mine it sure isn't." Merry paused and tried to focus on the right things to say. It was difficult considering the pounding inside her head. "I also owe you a debt of gratitude for keeping my deeds in the dark. Not many people would do that."

Mitch scowled and shook his head. "You owe your brother for that gift. He made sure everything pointed to him as the killer and finagled things so I'd come out a hero cop. Too bad the last part was a waste of time since I quit."

"You did? When?"

"Before the funeral. Couldn't stomach being called a hero cop by the press or another minute around Detective Hudson without beating him to a bloody pulp. My captain tried to talk me out of it, but I was adamant. I'm done with law enforcement."

"So, what's next?"

Mitch sighed. "Not a clue."

"You know, I didn't decide to go on a killing spree simply because of a tumor in my head. I wanted justice for my son and husband. If my doctor ever found out what I've done, he would probably say the mass skewed my moral compass. Maybe, maybe not. Doesn't really matter to me. What mattered, what drove me, was getting rid of as many dealers as possible. Do what I could in hopes another family didn't go through the same pain. The drive is still inside me; unfortunately, my body has other ideas."

Mitch let a small grin tug at the corners of his mouth. "You are one tough chick. I sure wouldn't mess with you."

"I used to be, but not anymore. I...don't have much longer, Mitch. I can feel it. You know, the worst part about dying now is I haven't been able to finish what I started. That's where I hope you'll come in."

"Where I come in? What do you mean?"

Merry leaned closer and patted the binders. "Derek left me a lot of information about his supplier in Memphis. Personal information I doubt your detective friend even knows. The things inside these binders would make finding, and killing, the prick quite simple. More than anything, I want to do it. The harsh reality is I'm physically unable now."

Because the justice gods are no longer smiling down on me. I'm too weak.

Mitch raised an eyebrow. "Are you saying what I think you are?"

Leaning back, Merry smiled. "I think the reason we never connected is because we're alike. Both of us possess a dark side. A very dark side. I know your type, Mitch, because I'm just like you. Don't you crave revenge for what happened to Derek? Want to slip your fingers around the neck of the bastard who he bought drugs from? Do your part—without any interference of the law—to rid the streets of dope, even if it's short-lived?"

"It's a big leap from cop to vigilante."

"Yes, it is. If you decide to do it, all you need to know about your target is inside. There's also three other items I wanted you to have, whether you make the jump to the dark side or not."

"And they are?"

Merry pointed at the first binder. "One is Joshua's journal. I want you to read it and understand just exactly what you're fighting for. I wish I would have read through it sooner—things might have turned out differently if I had." She stopped, swallowing the lump of tears in her throat. "One is a key to my storage unit at Store-N-Go off I-30. The other is this."

Mitch stared at the keys in Merry's trembling hand. "I don't need a car, Merry..."

"These are to Joshua's bike. Ownership papers are inside the binder. I've already signed it over to you. Now..." Merry's voice failed.

Her throat clenched shut. Mitch's face disappeared, replaced by blackness. Pain tore through her mind, worse than she'd ever felt. Unable to control her limbs, Merry crumpled to the ground. She heard Mitch yell for Debbie while he knelt by her side, his presence felt yet unseen.

"Hang on, Merry. We'll get you to the hospital."

Summoning the last bit of strength she possessed to fight off the death seizure, Merry whispered. "No. Let me go. Do this, Mitch. For Joshua."

24

10:00 A.M. SATURDAY MORNING

"You okay?"

Debbie nodded, unable to speak. Her heart physically ached with overwhelming grief at the loss of her best friend. The funeral had been simple, intimate, and quaint, just as Merry had wanted. Though Debbie thought it morbid, she'd made sure the tombstone was engraved with the exact phrase Merry requested: *And Justice For All*. Reading it as she placed a fresh bouquet of roses next to the marker made her queasy. Debbie hadn't spoken since the last handful of dirt was placed over Merry's grave.

"Looks like Percy is happy to see you," Mitch remarked as the big dog licked Debbie's hand. "I'm glad he seems to have bonded with you."

Debbie wiped her nose while clearing her throat. "Guess we need each other at the moment. We both miss her so much..."

Debbie's sobs broke free. She felt Mitch guide her to the couch, his warm arm around her shoulders.

"Wish I knew what to say. I'm not good at things like this."

"Obviously, I'm not either," Debbie mumbled into Mitch's shoulder.

"No, you're doing what you should, which is grieving and letting your emotions out. Guys like me aren't wired that way. We express our sorrow in others ways, which I'm about to do. Alone."

Debbie raised her wet face toward Mitch's. "You're leaving? Now? I...sort of hoped you'd at least stay for lunch. Maybe have one last toast to Merry?"

Mitch stood and held out his hand to Debbie. "I have some things to take care of the next few days. I'll be back no later than Tuesday. How about I come by for dinner and bring some champagne? We'll give Merry a proper toast with some high-priced alcohol."

Through her tears, Debbie smiled. "Sounds like a plan. Barbeque ribs okay with you?"

Mitch stood in the doorway and laughed. "I'm a Southern boy, so what do you think?"

Debbie waved and watched Mitch's car until it disappeared. Shutting the door, she walked inside and straight to the couch. Percy jumped up next to her, showering her face with wet kisses.

"Come on, boy. Since I'm a full-time artist now, let's use our sadness to create something magnificent. I'm thinking a painting of a beautiful, red-haired woman and her dog at the water's edge on a sunny day, trees and a pond in the background. How about you?"

＊＊＊

Forty minutes after leaving Debbie, Mitch found himself at the front entrance to Store-N-Go. He punched in the access code he'd memorized from Merry's notes and waited for the gate to open. Once inside, he drove to the designated unit and parked.

When he opened the metal door, a sweet piece of machinery sat less than three feet away. He admired her lines, ran his hands over the smooth leather seat. To his right, he noticed a large, framed picture and moved closer. The portrait of the once happy family made Mitch's anger spike. He felt the heat of sadness and grief poke inside his gut.

Rather than puss out and start crying, Mitch grabbed the handlebars and pushed the bike out. Glancing at the storage unit, he realized it was practically empty.

And had enough room to park his car.

Decision made as to where his new life would take him, Mitch started humming. A few minutes later, saddlebags packed and helmet secured, Mitch shut and locked the metal door. The sweet purr of the Honda made him almost giddy while he waited for the gate to open so he could get things rolling.

Without looking back, Mitch signaled and merged onto Interstate 40, a huge grin hidden under the visor as he passed the sign: *Memphis – 142 miles.*

Merry...this is for you.

And just the beginning for me.

ABOUT THE AUTHOR

Award-winning and International bestselling author Ashley Fontainne is an avid reader of mostly the classics. Ashley became a fan of the written word in her youth, starting with the Nancy Drew mystery series. Stories that immerse the reader deep into the human psyche and the monsters lurking within us are her favorite reads.

Her short thriller entitled *Number Seventy-Five*, touches upon the sometimes dangerous world of online dating. *Number Seventy-Five* took home the BRONZE medal in fiction/suspense at the 2013 Readers' Favorite International Book Awards contest and is currently in production for a feature film (www.number75thmovie.com).

Ashley's paranormal thriller, *The Lie*, won the GOLD medal in the 2013 Illumination Book Awards for fiction/suspense and is also in production for a feature film entitled *Foreseen* (www.foreseenmovie.com).

The paranormal/southern gothic horror/suspense novel, *Growl*, released in January of 2015. The suspenseful mystery *Empty Shell* released in September of 2014. Ashley teamed up with her mother, Lillian Hansen, in her latest book, *Blood Ties – The Bonds Are Permanent*. The psychological thriller, *Whispered Pain* released October 13, 2015. To learn more about Ashley, visit her website at www.ashleyfontainne.com